IF YOU LIVE IN A SMALL HOUSE

The authenticity of Park's characters, their food, their clothes, their expressions, brings immigrant family life in Hawai'i poetically alive. Most poignant is the father with his WWII memories and losing his friends to suicide missions, and his fear that his son will be sent to Korea to fight enemies who "look like him." A compelling reading experience.

—Kiana Davenport, author of *Shark Dialogues* and *House of Many Gods*

Completely avoiding the trappings of noisy, multi-generational family melodrama, this rich psychological narrative instead delves into the private longings of these characters. Beautifully told, *If You Live in a Small House* is the work of a truly gifted writer.

—Chris McKinney, author of *The Tattoo* and *The Queen of Tears*

Park's modernist story *If You Live in a Small House* is an important and beautiful chronicle of American lives too little known to us. Park's stunning novella is capacious as is the story's tender heart.

—Min Jin Lee, author of *Free Food for Millionaires*

Sandra Park writes with a generosity and clarity of vision that is both great-hearted and splendidly unsentimental. Nothing escapes her gaze. The writing is fresh and urgent, the language lyrical, the characters alive and kicking on the page. An utterly compelling read from the very first sentence, *Small House* is an auspicious debut for one of America's most promising new writers.

—Alice LaPlante, author of *Method and Madness: The Making of a Story* and *Do Not Go Gentle* (2011)

A hauntingly beautiful prose poem that opens the door to a hidden world and a forgotten moment, *If You Live in a Small House* is thoughtful, tender, and not to be missed.

—Patricia O'Toole, author of *The Five of Hearts* and *When Trumpets Call*

Sandra Park blends action and reverie to evoke the texture and mood of postwar Hawai'i in the lives of one Korean immigrant family. Reading *If You Live in a Small House* is like standing in Keaniani Lane after dark, peeking through the windows of the "funny kind house."

—Mary Helen Stefaniak, author of *The Cailiffs of Baghdad, Georgia* and *The Turk and My Mother*

Mesmerizing. Park's language is magical—her precise, yet fable-like descriptions draw the reader into a world both new and familiar. When I finally set the book aside, I felt as if I was waking from a dream.

—Shawna Yang Ryan, author of *Water Ghosts*

A captivating portrait of an island family whose troubles and loves are a spicy mix of heartbreak, hilarity, and pure intoxication.

—Steve Stern, author of *The Wedding Jester* and *The Angel of Forgetfulness*

This lovely novella evokes a lush poetry of the everyday. I admire the perfect economy of Sandra Park's writing, its richness of character, and her decision not to examine the tsunami's destruction, but rather the eerie beauty of the withdrawn sea that precedes it. Gloria says of Dante, "Looking is loving: I could look at you all day long." The reader will feel a similar affection for the book.

—Paul Hoover, author of *Sonnet 56* and *Poems in Spanish*

Park's narrative enfolds the complexity of a multi-ethnic island community, the histories of Asian immigration and settlement, and the presence of the United States military without subsuming the central exploration of the family's private dreams and experiences. She has achieved a wonderful balance between these larger historical narratives and the interiority of her characters, and her writing offers a stunning example of how political and cultural questions can exist harmoniously with aesthetic and narrative mastery.

—Paul Lai, Asian American Literature,
University of St. Thomas, Minnesota

Sandra Park's novel is beautifully told. She is flawless in evoking the atmosphere of the early 1950s, when Kailua was still the country, the Korean Conflict taking sons and fathers who survived the previous war, prosperity a glimmer just visible on the horizon. With subtle humor and tender regard for her characters, Park brings to life an ohana-household with barely room enough for their desires, hopes, and losses. Suspended in the lull before the tsunami of statehood, between forgetfulness and anticipation, Park's lyrical novella is a small miracle of remembrance.

—Frank Stewart, editor of *Manoa Journal* and author of *By All Means*

In the tradition of Sandra Cisneros's *House on Mango Street* and Toshio Mori's *Yokohama, California,* Park's linked vignettes provide us with glimpses of her characters' everyday lives…but, like the white-bordered, period photographs that accompany them, remind us that much lies outside our field of vision. While we come to understand that most of her characters' dreams will go unfulfilled, and while we come to sympathize with their losses and yearning, Park's book ultimately asks us to consider what historical and social forces shape the community of 1950s Kailua.

—Floyd Cheung, American Studies / Asian-Am. Literature
Smith College

Character List

Mother and Father, local Koreans, raising four children and supporting an extended family of twelve under one roof. Father, a World War II veteran, misses his overseas mistress and goes fishing. Mother's capacious heart absorbs family members into their Kailua house, one by one.

Grandmother and Grandfather, Mother's parents who immigrated from Korea. As Grandmother serves Grandfather's every whim, she remembers her first husband, a dreamer who escaped their plantation life.

Gloria, Mother's middle-aged, unmarried sister. Longing for a husband and her own house, Gloria fixes her fantasies on Dante, the rubbish man, on his weekly pick-up runs along Keaniani Lane.

Dante, rubbish man by day, popular musician by night, love object among the neighborhood women. He mourns the loss of his brother in the war and misses his mother with deep, undying attachment.

Shorty and Fatso, Mother's and Gloria's brothers. Shorty, the smart one in the family, pursues a never-ending courtship with Eunice in Honolulu. Fatso is loyal to Shorty above all, while he rues a string of missed opportunities and that elusive Lady Luck.

Rene, a young bachelor cousin. Drifting from his family house to this one, he dreams of becoming an entertainer, a smooth-talking crooner.

Lana and Liz, eleven and ten years old, thought of as twins by the family. Lana directs their pretend play and Liz gladly submits to her sister's gift for drama—what lurks beneath the veil of domesticity.

Ezra, seven. The only boy, he is the designated golden child. Although far too young for service in the Korean War, he inherits an idea of valor that leads to mischief and, then, to a world away from home.

Lucy, a toddler—a sturdy child, affectionately passed around like a sack of rice.

IF YOU LIVE IN A SMALL HOUSE

Sandra Park

Mutual Publishing

An earlier version of Chapters Eight and Nine appeared in *The Iowa Review* under the title "Another Warning."

Photos used by permission of owner (see Photo Credits, p. 171).

"Panini Puakea," used by permission of Alfred Music Publishing Co., Inc.
Music and Lyrics by John Kamealoha Almeida, Arranged by Johnny Noble © 1989 (Renewed) EMI Miller Catalog Inc. All rights administered by EMI Miller Catalog Inc. (Publishing) and Alfred Publishing Co., Inc. (Print). All Rights Reserved.

"I Didn't Know What Time It Was," used by permission of Alfred Music Publishing Co., Inc.
Lyrics by Lorenz Hart, Music by Richard Rodgers © 1939 (Renewed) by Chappell & Co. Rights for extended renewal term in U.S. controlled by W.B. Music Corp. and Williamson Music. All Rights Reserved.

"Fly Me To The Moon (In Other Words)," used by permission.
Words and Music by Bart Howard. TRO-© Copyright 1954 (Renewed) Hampshire House Publishing Corp., New York, NY.

Design by Jane Gillespie
First Printing, September 2010
ISBN-10: 1-56647-927-4
ISBN-13: 978-1-56647-927-1

Library of Congress Cataloging-in-Publication Data

Park, Sandra, 1948-
  If you live in a small house / Sandra Park.
    p. cm.
  ISBN-13: 978-1-56647-927-1 (alk. paper)
  ISBN-10: 1-56647-927-4 (alk. paper)
  1. Korean American families--Fiction. 2. Oahu (Hawaii)--Fiction. 3. Hawaii--History--1900-1959--Fiction. 4. Domestic fiction. I. Title.
  PS3616.A74365I36 2010
  813'.6--dc22
                                    2010021846

Mutual Publishing, LLC
1215 Center Street, Suite 210
Honolulu, Hawai'i 96816
Ph: (808) 732-1709
Fax: (808) 734-4094
e-mail: info@mutualpublishing.com
www.mutualpublishing.com

Printed in Korea

For my parents,

Lily and Harry Park

Jean's Bakery off Oneawa Street.

Contents

Striking sugar workers.

Acknowledgments

For their patience and kindness, I wish to thank my teachers—Sheila Donohue for early encouragement, Peter Weltner who taught me how to read closely, and special thanks to Maxine Chernoff for her prompt responses from the heart.

As a musician and writer, Michael Maisonpierre gave his time and close attention. And deep thanks to James Brook and Nathan Wirth who guide my reading to new places.

For lifting the spirit, this daring and dauntless posse always comes to the rescue—Geri Ihara, Janice Ing Strauss, Alejandra Chaverri—any day, any time.

And mahalo to Tom Farber, who helps writers find a home for their book manuscripts—under his care, a long list of homes and books.

Finally, this book was saved from ten more years of dust mites by Gavan Daws, a lifelong friend of writers—nobody smarter, funnier, more generous has yet jumped out of the bushes.

Writing, a selfish, obsessive pursuit, often takes away from those close by—so, endless love to my children, Naomi, David, and Sarah, and to my husband, John.

About the Photographs

You are invited to enter the world of *If You Live in a Small House* by way of an array of photographs evoking the fifties in Hawai'i.

That era seems long ago and far away now—a time when days passed slowly and quietly in the warmth of the sun, when family life was lived comfortably among friends and neighbors, and when nobody was thinking much about the big world outside and all the turbulent changes that might be coming to Hawai'i.

People who looked through the camera viewfinder then did not see the future. They saw what they had always seen around them. They liked what they saw, clicked the shutter, took the film to be developed at the drugstore, and pasted their snapshots in family albums with handwritten captions. This was all before home video, long before cell phones—and it was all in black and white.

Looking at those nostalgic still photos now—fifty years on, two generations later—we can transport ourselves back in time, into the world of the people of this story, the family who lived in a small house on a narrow lane in a modest suburb on the windward side of Oʻahu. Their world becomes our world too.

The photos have been gathered from public and private sources. Randy and Mike Groza of the Kailua Historical Society put us in touch with the families and collectors who contributed photos to the Society's excellent book, *Kailua,* including George and Lynn Abe, Erling William Hedemann, Jr., and Trudi Miyaji.

The *Honolulu Star-Bulletin,* now the *Honolulu Star-Advertiser,* kindly shared file photos. The City and County of Honolulu made available photos of city workers. Bishop Museum and the Hawaiʻi State Archives were other sources. Photos also came from the Samuel Lee Collection and the Dr. Jackie Young Collection. And Carl Hebenstreit was kind enough to furnish a photo of Kini Popo. Our thanks to them all.

Detailed photo credits are on page 171.

— *Editor*

Coconut grove, Kailua.

Prologue

According to neighbors, Father was a difficult man. He did not talk much, pulling down his mouth as if considering something important. But everyone agreed that if something is important, it's either in the *Honolulu Star-Bulletin* or, at the very least, the talk of the town. Their salty neighbor was probably just making things up in his head, constructing thoughts as inconsequential as cigarette smoke, diminishing their fellow feeling. Nothing galls friendly neighbors more than the stubborn silence of another, setting itself apart from sunny greetings and daily gossip. The man's muteness seemed to suggest that everybody else was playfully splashing around in bubbly, shallow waters, the safety of white foam on white sands, too much at ease in the island's heat and humidity. The man's stillness gathered around him, enlarging the space between him and others.

After too many beers, other men made vows to publicly insult their silent neighbor while their wives claimed that nobody, not a single one, could resist the latest news, Arthur Godfrey is coming to town! With his hit songs and ukulele!

Almost everybody had a television or knew somebody who had one. There was so much to be glad about—the boys home from the European and Pacific fronts, GI loans for houses and cars. Now it was war in Korea, with General MacArthur flying in and out, saluting on the tarmac of Hickam Field, predicting victory.

After years of curfew and blackouts, local folks were ready to start over, find a way to make do with what was left, joke about how good Spam and rice tasted with the right seasonings. Only in their beds, out of earshot of their children, did grownups wonder out loud. Why Korea? Was this some kind of unfinished business? Why were we fighting on the ground, letting them stick our boys?

An island in the middle of the ocean is a small world. Ancient Hawaiians prayed for stasis, the counterpoise of dark brown land and bright blue water, wishing only for the give and take of the tides to continue as before, even as we sleep. Radio, television, even the neighbors' relentless commentary on Keaniani Lane and all of its inhabitants, scrambled words until all was noise, nothing Father could read or pronounce. It took packs of cigarettes and occasional strong drink to let it all go. After all, even a proud man must unlock his stiff neck before going to bed. Like the ox who lowers his head to submit to the yoke, this man allowed his wife to take his heavy head onto her breast.

He lived in a small, crowded house. The best he could do was pull the shades, go fishing.

Neighbors talked among themselves, sipping instant coffee. That man came back from the war in Europe with no stories to tell. How was it possible to go so far away and return empty handed? When he was in Italy, did he eat spaghetti? Say "Ciao, baby"? What about his buddies? He did not speak of the war, even after heavy food and drink.

Not only that, he did not fish with respect for the sport. Instead of live bait and casting into the sea, he seeded his waters with bread bombs, setting up easy pickings for the next day. A real fisherman would not do this. Bread bombs attract huge swirls of otherwise restless, wily fish, tempting them to stick around for more. What happened to the notion of hard work and honesty in all things? Who was he kidding? And his family was in on it—he even taught his son how to make bombs.

Their house was an embarrassment to the neighborhood. Tickytacky additions. Yellowed front yard. And a pink cement driveway. Neighbors were looking for more, quoting the governor, "a better life in beautiful Hawai'i." Only a fool would argue with swaying palm trees and clear skies. And the children were getting taller, smarter than their parents. The aloha spirit was rising, friendly word-of-mouth almost guaranteed some kind of happiness. Far above the islands, the great gyre gathered speed, a beneficent first cause of gentle rain and cooling trade winds. Some said it was God's breath moving across the waters.

But war had accelerated and multiplied everything; there was so much out there. No longer did anyone remember or bother to wish for a small peaceable kingdom. And this fool? He looked like a fool—in baggy pants and holey shirt, a dumb work horse, unyielding to the good news of the day.

Children playing.

Fishing for tilapia on Kawainui Stream.

Bread on the Driveway

ow upon row, slices of bread covered the driveway. It took a whole day to dry both sides of the bread. Father deemed it ready when he could feel the crumbs, like dry points of color, barely held together by the machine shape of the loaf. Sitting on a low stool, he took one slice at a time, rubbing it between his hands, sifting a stream of fine crumbs into a clean bucket.

Although he did this each week of every summer, the neighbor children would watch this slow, methodical job as if they had not seen anything like it. A big boy held the shoulders of his younger brother in front of him. Only the man's son, Ezra, was allowed to touch the bread. All arms and legs, the skinny boy lined up the white bread on the pink cement, sprawling dramatically whenever he adjusted a row to line up with the others. In all the summers of doing this, the sky stayed pale and hot without a drop of rain. All the same, Mother asked the same question whenever Father started the job, "What if it rains? There goes the bread, there goes the bread money." To which he replied, "It's not going to rain."

Everybody at Piggly Wiggly Market knew father and son, their cart filled to the brim with loaves of the local brand, Love's Bread, in red gingham plastic, the same crackly plastic that snugly fit over Lucky Strike cigarette packs. Father tapped each cigarette on the Lucky red target before hanging it from his mouth, unlit. Ezra looked for the checkout lane with his Auntie Gloria, hers was usually the long, slow line because she chatted with the customers. "There she is, c'mon!" While the line snaked along, Father looked at naked girls in *Playboy.* The women in line tried to start a conversation with the man, but he preferred the glossy pictures to the real ones with kerchiefs tied over their pin curls. The boy, half as tall as his father, could not see the picture of Miss July, "red hot, true blue, and pure white...she can't resist a man in uniform, a true patriot from Pine Bluff, Arkansas." The boy asked for chewing gum, his father replied, "Uh-huh." Happy with the bounce of chicle in his mouth, the boy patiently nudged the cart forward.

"Attaboy!" Gloria greeted the boy as if she hadn't seen him in years. She lived in the same house, their house, in a room that was once the front porch. Father

Kailua Market.

fixed it up with solid walls and two small windows. "Until she gets married," he said. Gloria was fifty-one years old, but the family said she looked surprisingly young for her age. She said her hair stayed black because she used a special tonic and massaged her scalp every day. Her hair was combed smooth on top, forming a fluffy, optimistic flip at the ends. Unlike other ladies, Gloria slept with her pin curls. "It's not that bad once you get used to it." Her tonics, creams and unguents kept her fresh and ready.

Gloria was mother's sister. Although Father and Gloria did not get along, the days and years unfurled with few visible disagreements. In his estimation, she talked too much and spent too much money on herself. The square white house on Keaniani Lane was sagging with the weight of four children, grandparents, Gloria, two uncles, and extra cousins, including sad, beautiful Rene. There were only two real bedrooms, but father had converted other spaces into extra rooms.

Whenever he had too much to drink, he kidded Uncle Fatso that he should pay rent for his "double wide load." Uncle Shorty, loyal to Fatso, paid for expensive treats, like restaurant roast duck. Boy Scouts marveled at the quantities of Portuguese *pao duce,* sweet bread that Uncle Shorty bought when they came to the door, selling for the next big Makahiki, the statewide scout roundup in Honolulu. At the dinner table, Uncle

Robert "Lucky" Luck.

Shorty made the kids laugh, imitating Lucky Luck on television. "Ummm, 'ono good," he growled with pleasure as he broke the round loaf of *pao duce*. A local star, Lucky Luck wore a frayed straw hat and an aloha shirt too small to button over his belly. He interviewed local guests, usually nightclub singers and chefs with secret recipes. Of course, island people knew that the secret to chicken adobo is plain white vinegar "for that extra kick." But, Lucky Luck made a big deal out of it, wheedling the secret out of Chef Fang, from a top Waikiki hotel.

Uncle Shorty made up for everything, he was mother's older brother and the smartest one of all. His heartbreak was that girls didn't care if he was smart. His girlfriend, Eunice, led a separate life in town. He loved her, so the family said nothing.

After the war, the islands were booming. Father had returned from Italy with his head attached to his shoulders, changed but not ruined. He reunited with his wife. Without the occasion of a homecoming, however, he could have mistaken another woman for his wife, her face had merged with other faces from overseas. He remembered her as willowy with wavy hair touching her shoulders. Instead, he saw a stocky woman with short, curly hair. She said that worry made her eat and that her Tony home perm treatment would eventually "relax."

Now that he was safely home, things would be different. The family draped yellow plumeria lei around his neck. Their heavy scent made his stomach sick. He smiled broadly and gave a lei to each lady in the crowded room, kissing the young ones on the lips. Gloria wondered aloud why she just got a peck on the cheek. As requested, he kissed her on the lips, a reluctant kiss that seemed to sink into her painted, fleshy lips. Then he kissed a young girl, a cousin's daughter from the far side of the island, to keep the flame alive. Far away from home, he had sought consolation from strangers. He grew up with the notion that only Hawai'i people know the meaning of love and family, but he learned otherwise. Perfect strangers turned out to be roughly equal parts kind and cruel, like his family at home. After losing most of the soldiers he knew on suicide missions, he could have stayed overseas and started a new life.

Far from home, he could be anybody, nothing would surprise him. He no longer could tell the difference between a good girl and a bad girl because they dreamed about the same things. Foreign girls don't talk about fooling around, stealing other people's money. Like the girls back home, they dream about keeping house for a family, inventing new ways to save money for Christmas.

Looking for U.S. dollars, *signorinas* were wandering the streets, on a mission to save their families and rescue the best years of their lives. It only took a cigarette to start a conversation, a few friendly words, talking with hands to indicate how many years since birth, miles away from home, hours until dawn. A fat girl with blue eyes would laugh with her mouth wide open: he could see her tongue curl and uncurl, her breath scented with sour milk. The girls back home covered their mouths when they laughed because their mothers had taught them modesty, even their eyes seemed effaced, lids lowered like pull shades. A foggy vision he struggled to recollect, a laughing girl swam into view, eyes wide, mouth open, its pink insides exposed, shameless. Over a year-long tour of duty, he had lived several lifetimes of romance, the collapsed cycles of love and loss in times of war.

Back in the islands, everyone in the family strummed their own private ukuleles, weak with relief or lost in grief, except Father. He studied papers for a postwar house loan. One of his old girlfriends worked in a bank, showing him tables of payments and interest rates. He picked a long-term steady rate spread over a lifetime. The numbers, the big money involved made him suddenly feel like an old man.

Coconut Grove in Kailua was an up and coming town, over the Pali, the steep cliffs of the windward side of O'ahu. There wasn't much there yet, but a star pattern of streets radiated from the town's old banyan tree. The tree screeched with black mynah birds, its branches reaching for more light as its dangling roots gathered below, a heavy skirt of respectability. Old men sat under the banyan, commenting on the new cars with sloping backs and sharp fins—Packards, Edsels, Studebakers, so much traffic for such a little town.

Miss July played on father's mind as he finished sifting dry bread through his fingers. He wanted a patriotic gal, another house, with no more than two children, no pets. A fresh start, he could work one job instead of two, kiss his children good night, swing on the porch with Miss July. He liked Italian girls too, the way they walked in dresses and two-toned sandals. If he had to choose between Miss July and Sophia, kicking her leg up to flounce her skirt, he would pick Sophia. Once she got over the fact that he could be slanty eyed and an American at the same time, they had had a good time. She played with his dog tags, warm from their place inside his shirt. He bought her drinks and gave her American dollars. She lived in an apartment with too many relatives and a few strangers. The strangers were supposed to pay rent, but they had no money. Running his hands through the bucket of crumbs, he laughed at himself. Sophia in Turin, his wife in Kailua, it was the same. He always fell for the girl with the big heart.

"Water?" His wife set down a tin pail. He looked up at her. Hoping for more, she paused, swatting a fly.

He plunged his hands into the water, then started to build a snowball of breadcrumbs. "You have the touch, honey," she said. Plunging and patting, he carefully made three large balls of breadcrumbs.

The small crowd of children waited for Ezra to wave them over for a look. They passed in single file along the edge of the driveway, modestly avoiding the invisible center line that belonged to the father and son, the younger ones peering into the bucket, the older looking over their shoulders. It was not exactly a miracle, but it was extraordinary to see innumerable slices of bread reduced to three snowy bread balls. Pressed into shape with wet hands, their toasty fragrance had disappeared into a hidden center. The children continued to murmur, point, and look to their heart's content. In the years to come, they would remember the smell of bread on hot concrete, the back-and-forth movement of a boy laying out and collecting bread, their tough bare feet absorbing the rising heat, all of which will later instruct them on the cycles of hunger and thirst, the relentless motion of particles, and above all, the paths of light that circle the air, unseen only because of the glaring sun.

Mother brought out a beer and watched her husband drink it. "More?" After the second bottle, he kissed her on the lips. The children being as peaceable as plants, the husband and wife felt easy about showing their affection.

Father got into the Morris Minor and backed slowly out of the driveway. The children stepped aside and dispersed, the youngest waving to the friendly face of the sputtering automobile. The bread balls were nestled into one another, the bucket flat on the floor in front of the passenger seat, where the driver could keep an eye on them.

The small car chugged along two-lane Kalaniana'ole Highway, moving over whenever a faster, sleeker car rode its tail. At first, the funny little car was the laughingstock of the family, but father said it was built for comfort, not for speed, just like Mother. He had pictured the two of them in the front seats, a picnic basket in the back, heading to the beach or a drive-in movie. Instead, he usually rode in it alone or with his son, since she always wanted to bring the kids and Gloria and there wasn't enough room for everyone.

Leaving Kailua Bay for Waimanalo Bay was like leaving town for country. Waimanalo was wet and green with squatters' huts and beach camps dotting the shore. Turning onto a dirt road, the Morris Minor made sputtering sounds, its small wheels fitting nicely into the same ruts of other wheels. A bare-chested boy waved happily. Father bounced slowly along the road, tossing down an espresso with Sophia after a lazy morning. Italians open their throats and toss back liquor, sauce, love. Fortunately, mother liked Italian movies so they

Newly built Kalanianaole Highway.

could watch the show and travel separately to smoky cafes and narrow attic beds. "Sophia, Sophia, Sophia," the little car chugged, passing one more hut and two chickens, pecking at dirt. Father didn't like the way the car's motion and thoughts of love were juggling the restless boys in his pants. So he stopped and parked on the side of the road. Why not carry the bucket and walk the rest of the way, he thought to himself. The bare-chested boy reappeared and offered to wash his car. "Okay, son." The boy skipped away, yelling for a pail of water. Father could hear other boys calling back and wondered if he had enough change in his pocket for all of them. Even the chickens seemed overexcited by new prospects.

Dusk came earlier to this side of the bay with its thicker foliage creeping toward the beach. The man walked the length of the broken-down pier. Beyond the AT YOUR OWN RISK sign, he walked with memory in his feet. He knew where the slats were missing, which boards creaked loudly but held fast. Near the end, he set down the bucket. After all these years, it was a wonder that nobody in the small boy's hut or the chicken house had discovered this spot. He could see the mullet running below, silvery smooth fish known as nibblers who outfoxed most fishermen. As fickle as girls, the mullet could gently nibble bait off a line without getting hooked. That is, unless they got greedy. The green waves made a racket against the old blackened pilings. Water rushed, slammed, split into many waves, shooting up foam. As the pier swayed and creaked, the man tossed out three bread balls, plunking them at strategic intervals near the pier strut below, where he would sit the next day, pole fishing.

He walked away without watching the mullet swirl excitedly, flailing against each other for the bait.

Countryside Windward O'ahu.

A post-war Kailua house.

Inside a Cedar Chest

Father pushed his chair away from the table, looking at his wife, moving a toothpick around in his mouth. He could flip it sideways, vertically touch the roof of his mouth, shoot it out his lips, suck it back in, flip again. Not a big talker, he cultivated his own art form. When Ezra started to mimic his father's toothpick routine, Mother hit the roof. "Don't do that! We want you to study, go to college!" A smart boy, all he could think about was how long it would take him to learn the toothpick trick.

The mullet haul was huge, two five-gallon buckets of mature, sleek fish. The table was littered with their clean, perfect skeletons. It was the family way to pick at a mullet without disturbing a single white bone.

Thrilled with the catch, Mother had grilled a thick red steak with a pile of onion rings for her husband. While everyone picked at fish bones, Father methodically sawed away at his juicy steak, dipping each piece in a homemade mess of ketchup, Worcestershire, and Tabasco. He drank two bottles of beer while everyone else had plain water out of the tap. Whenever Uncle Fatso or Uncle Shorty complained, Father raised his eyebrows at Mother. Then she reminded an uncle, usually Fatso, that it was all her fault, ever since the day she packed bananas with Father's lunch to eat on the pier.

Everyone knows that taking bananas on a fishing trip is bad luck; she didn't know what she was thinking when she did this. Anyway, the sight of the bananas, even the thought of bananas, killed Father's taste for fish. Both uncles said this made no sense, but Mother said, "Don't be jealous, be grateful." Fatso was unmoved. He silently opened and closed his mouth each time Father tucked a dripping piece of meat into his mouth. Ezra thought his uncle looked like a fish, a slow moving bottom fish, a brown tilapia burrowing for scraps. That's how it was with the boy, his heart staunchly loyal to his father.

Auntie Gloria rose in a flurry. She felt oceans of sympathy for her younger brothers, convinced that her sister's husband ruled the house with too much iron.

The men moved to the patio to cool off.

Gloria disappeared into the bathroom. She filled the deep claw-footed tub almost to the brim, adding a cup of Epsom salts and rose water. Through the door, she could hear her old father loudly comment on his dinner tray, carried to his room by her married sister, trailed by their old mother, apologizing in Korean for the bones in the fish, secretly hoping a long, sharp one would lodge sideways in her husband's throat. Two bad luck marriages, Gloria thought. Humming *"... I never knew what time it was / till there was you..."* she soaked up to her chin. The steamy mist would open her pores, sweating ugly little toads that would hop away, springing on their brown-freckled hind legs, to the land of grudges and regrets. She pinched her nose, immersed herself wholly, counted to ten. Breaking surface, she felt like a baby in a baptismal font. She had read in a magazine that grudges and regrets left furrows and potholes on the face. Better to melt like a pat of butter, sweet and golden. Sweating, her lips slightly parted, she wished the roses in the water were real, floating petals instead of an invisible essence. The rose infusion in the blue pharmacy bottle was expensive, its label claiming that it contained armloads of damask roses, cut at the height of their bloom.

She pulled up the rubber stopper, the tub gurgled long and loud, announcing to the back of the house just how much hot water was going down the drain. But she didn't care. Tomorrow was rubbish day and she would see Dante. Or, as she preferred to think of it, Dante would see her. She rubbed her feet with an old towel, roughly. Tomorrow she would wear open-toe sandals, a dainty size five.

From where he sat, Father could see his wife through venetian blinds, a figure moving in horizontal stripes of light, pulling apart and mingling like water, tricking the eye. It looked like she was painting the dishes with swirls of color and Grandmother was drying and dropping plates, making sorrowful noises whenever one would crash to the floor. Mother swept up the pieces. He didn't understand why his wife let her old mother break everything in the house.

Their two girls, Liz and Lana, sat on the sofa, watching television. The family called them twins even though they were born almost a year apart. The youngest, Lucy, crawled into the kitchen. Mother picked up the baby and took her outside to the patio, handing her over to Father, "Broken glass." For the rest of the evening, Father and the uncles made sure Lucy stayed aloft, safe from the rubble in the kitchen. The baby was good and quiet with Uncle Fatso because she could climb him.

At ages eleven and twelve, the twins were straying away from their mother (who reminded them of unnecessary things to do), toward their resident auntie (who took their side against the rest of the world). For a time, on the cusp of adolescence, they were ceaseless observers of their Auntie Gloria. Although they would eventually grow up to make fun of their unmarried auntie, these days they could think of nothing better to do than visit Gloria in her tiny room.

That evening, as usual, the girls sat on a carved cedar chest behind their auntie's dresser. The chest held things in safekeeping: fine cotton pillow cases edged with crocheted points, crocheted doilies and a long runner for a table, pressed and folded handkerchiefs, two blue and white summer kimonos, two pairs of slippers woven with sandy green straw, two hair brushes with real boar bristles, and at the bottom, tipping like an anchor into white bath towels, a crystal punch bowl with twelve cups and a curved ladle. Interleaved in the layers of cloth were silver fish scorpions, black commas and curlicues with barbed seraphs in broken lines, their shiny dried trails of scum leaving a mark on each layer of new, unworn clothing.

An arbor of peach trees with two strolling figures was deeply carved into the top of the chest. Tilting the mirror on its hinges, Gloria could tend to herself and talk to the twins at the same time. Lana passed bobby pins one at a time from a heart-shaped candy box. "… seven, eight, nine!" It would be time to get a haircut when Gloria could wind her hair more than ten times around her finger, a flat circle of hair to be affixed to her tender scalp with two crisscrossed bobby pins. By the time she was done, her neck ached and her eyebrows arched a bit more sharply from the pulling pins. Lana patted the tight wet head in sympathy, gently pulling on the exposed ear lobes, "Auntie, your head is perfect... like arithmetic!"

In slow circles, Gloria massaged her cheeks with cold cream, dipping and applying the white cream to her forehead in overlapping circles, closing her eyes, her face shiny, a waxed apple on a stick. Wiping off the excess with tissue, her face reappeared. Leaning into the mirror, she checked for signs of age or worry. Gloria's expression often reminded the girls of a baby's, open and friendly without a hint of experience. A mask of serenity protected her soft face: linen soaked in salt can stop an arrow. A daub of cream on the elbows completed the ritual. The girls each dipped into the cream, putting dots of white on one another's small faces. What about the rest of Auntie Gloria, they wondered, each part, all the shades of tan and pink skin? When Gloria raised her arms to her head, Lana could see clear up the kimono sleeve to her armpits. She knew that her auntie pinched her nipples every morning as part of her wake-up routine. She told the girls that facial exercises and pinching kept her younger than springtime. By the time the girls had to leave for bed, they carried bright red impressions of Gloria's cedar chest on the backs of their thighs. Their faces were placid mirrors of each other, unaware of the angry streaks on their backsides.

Something knocked on Gloria's high window, a soft trade wind, the casual knock of a visitor. She reached up and opened the window, the night air shocking her wet scalp. Looking out the high window or into the mirror, the room didn't feel as small as it was—she and the sky shared an inky black mystery. When she pictured herself in this house, she saw a set of nesting boxes, one box fitting neatly into another, and another, and another. Her room was a box: inside was herself and her reflected image. Inside her self were separate jewel boxes for her memories and her heart. Growing up in the Honolulu house, in her own blue-papered room, she lolled around without a sense of where she was or what she was doing. Now she knew with an adult sense of certainty that she was inhabiting a strict, unforgiving space: the place of a maiden aunt in her married sister's house.

Grandmother dropped two more glasses, one full of water. Mother mopped up, her baby riding piggyback. Rene walked into the house, looking at the women, looking away, unfolding his thin frame onto the sofa. He closed his eyes, listening to the women speculate (for his pleasure) on his bachelor whereabouts.

"Rene's as free as a bird."

"Going everywhere."

"Wonder where."

"It's not for us to know."

The shuffle of the women's cloth house slippers felt like music to Rene, like the rhythmic slapping of water against the side of a boat, a small boat moored in shallow water, each tug followed by relaxation.

Gloria waited for everyone to go to bed before she padded over to the darkened kitchen. Empty and silent, the kitchen looked strange, like anybody's kitchen with the blank faces of cupboards and counter tops. The Frigidaire hummed like a space ship. She measured a full glass of milk then emptied it into a soup bowl. First dipping her toes into the bowl, she washed each foot in milk, soaking up its fatty white liquid, then patting her toes dry with a thin dish cloth. She folded the cloth and returned it to the rim of the sink (her feet were cleaner than the dishes). Closing the door silently, she walked outside. The last drops of milk were sprinkled over bare ground under the low avocado tree. The small bones of her pet cat lay below. She believed that her sister's husband killed the cat because he detested the thought of one more mouth to feed. Sophia, a gray and white long hair with a question mark plume for a tail, had been her confidante. Together they had talked about the mysteries of life, matters of the heart.

Before Dante, there had been others, the man who took the time to answer her questions about home appliances and the Sears guarantee. After a number of visits, she settled on an automatic toaster for her sister,

money "like water." Only Grandmother felt satisfied because she had sent a large check to her family in Korea, a sum equal to immortal tales about her new life in America. Grandfather said his sons were spoiled and unwilling to work. It wasn't clear what happened to the rest of the money and nobody wanted to talk about it. The big Honolulu house had gone up in smoke.

At first, Gloria and her brothers would bring home gifts every day, special items for the new house—the living room filled up with stuffed chairs, a coffee table, a record player, then, a television in a large wooden cabinet. Ezra got a new toy every day. They started as talkative, overly cheery visitors and eventually stayed on as more sullen fixtures of the household.

Mother's family members presented themselves as a plumbing problem, slow seepage that established a permanent map of stains across the floor plan of the small Kailua house. Territory was established by habit: in the early years, Gloria slept with Grandmother and the girls; Fatso and Shorty camped out with Grandfather and Ezra.

The living room sofa belonged to Rene after the television was switched off. Rene drifted in and out of the scene, a lost boy who had wandered from his house to theirs. He wanted to be an entertainer, maybe a singer or master of ceremonies, leading a night life. Mother remembered him as a baby born too early, a scrawny little thing that couldn't keep up with the rest of the world. No one in the family ever saw him eat. He slept in his clothes and seemed to evaporate into the hustle and bustle of the day. Once in a while he would be gone for a spell, then show up as if he hadn't ever left.

A half-moon casts a ghost light on everything, outlining the dark edge of a leaf, a glowing wash tub propped against a wall. The night air feels like a second bath, a cool drenching with a soft breeze. Gloria kneels beside the avocado tree, trailing a finger in the dirt under it. In the half-light she looks like a young penitent, shaved and robed, a small bowed head, flowing sleeve dragging on the ground.

Inside, Father lies awake in bed. He feels like a strong drink but stays put, staring at the ceiling. The changing pattern of light reminds him of shallow foaming water shot with green. He adored night when he was a boy: drawn into the larger scale of night and stars, he felt older than his years; the endlessness of the night sky filled his boy's chest with wonder: he saw a sky laden with stars and he thought he could see what was holding up the vault of darkness, the strong-arm scaffolding of cold air, compressed, moving in upward and downward spirals, passing one another along the way. One night when he was his son's age, he thought the stars in their plenitude were coalescing, dripping light, shedding their light all around him. He wanted to run and tell the world that it was as bright as noon in the middle of the night. No longer a boy, he still loved night but the dark sky felt endless without beneficence. He loved the night sky because he could remember it, not because he continued to see what he saw as a boy. If a man lost his love for night, he could drown in his own conclusions, his eyes filling, ears stopped, throat closing.

A City and County of Honolulu refuse truck.

From the Hedge to the Street

Connecting the dots from Gloria's bedroom window to the hedge to the street formed a shallow, acutely slanting triangle that took in the street with a wide lens, a fish-eye that brought Dante closer to her, floating large in a foreground of breadfruit and leaves.

This view was so familiar and fixed in Gloria's mind that she thought of the street and hedge as a sign of cohabitation, the side by side positions of husband and wife. If life was nothing without love, Gloria and Dante belonged to one another. Love was a three-fold mystery: Gloria's love for Dante, Dante's obliviousness to her love, and the possibility of discovery. The possibility that something in the air could change existed as long as they were both alive, going about in tandem rhythms, swept up, bending low. She had wished for a picture window so she could sit in an upholstered chair, looking out serenely. Father said that a picture window was the same as a sign that said open for business, a remark that kept her quiet for days.

Since the original porch space was a three-by-five foot rectangle, Father had built it up, adding shelves and a slatted window near the top to admit light but maintain privacy. It resembled a cell with a high ceiling. The end of the bed pushed a foot or so into the living room, a leg of space defined by a low wall, as if the rest of the bed were a storefront display case. By draping a scarf near the end of the bed where a wall would be, Gloria could sleep in relative peace. When the porch bedroom was first completed, it was a novelty: the girls would sneak up to the low wall and point to their auntie's disembodied legs, the lady sawed in two, now you see her, now you don't!! Everyone took a look before going to bed, Fatso wagged her big toe affectionately and called yoohoo until his sleepy sister told him to shut up. A curtain of beads separated Gloria's bedroom from the living room. During the day the room was too sunny and hot, the beads sparkling amber and green. Otherwise, it was an improvement for the living room that was now always dim and cool, ideal for naps and television viewing.

As in most crowded homes, people learned how to draw the shade, looking and seeing nothing. Gloria's room was no longer a novelty, except to the occasional wide-eyed visitor who tried to squint a look inside. Along the length of time, it developed its own dimensions, an alcove of cold fluid statuary, red votive candles, discarded gold and silver foil, reserved for its own sake. No one bothered to look and thus the spirit gathered in its confines.

Waking from dreams smelling of vanilla, baby Lucy opened her eyes in slow flaps, kicking the wooden bars of her crib. One side of the crib was let down to provide a low railing in case she rolled over but easy enough to climb down. Grandmother slept in the royal sarcophagus position, on her back with her arms folded across her chest. The twins slept together in a single bed, their arms and legs interlocked, dreaming the same dream. Lucy toddled then crawled on all fours down the hall to her parents' bed.

Mother released the pins of Lucy's sagging diaper, letting it drop to the floor, felt the wet lower edge of her T-shirt and pulled that off, then hauled her into bed. The baby clung to her mother's warm softness, fitting neatly into the wide C of her body, returning to her dreams of vanilla, that breath scent of milk. Father rolled toward the wall and rocked back. It was the time of sweetest sleep, in the cool dark hours before dawn and the first blast of heat. If one could linger in that blue light, neither asleep or awake, the possibility of dreams could rise with the heat, gaining loft as it grows in size, a friendly blue cloud that sheds love on ordinary things. When the blue cloud turns white and fluffy, drifting across the sky, love is gone and the weather takes over.

By the time Gloria walked home from a day's work, she was exhausted, weighed down by a bag of groceries and light sleep from the night before. It was just as well that rubbish day came around only once a week to allow a cycle of rest and anticipation. The passing sight of Dante jogging next to the truck, upending densely packed rubbish cans as if they were paper cups, required a focus of looking that could take in his whole working figure, arms and legs going all at once, as well as a closer look at his face, how his long hair blew back in gleaming crimps above a wide forehead, his eyes dark and hooded beneath a jutting brow bone, his mouth turned down with purpose.

Like a number of other rubbish men, Dante was also a musician, playing slack key guitar at weddings and first birthday lū'au. Gloria had wanted to ask him to play at Ezra's first birthday (she would pay for it) (maybe she and Dante could sing a little duet or he could sing and she could do an impromptu hula) but her sister's brother said that was out of the question. Instead, they had plenty of food but no music. "If we have music nobody will ever go home." Uncle Fatso chimed in, "When the Hawaiians have parties, nobody goes home. They eat, take a nap, eat some more, dance around, drink, fall down, keep on going for days!" Dante's reputation was local, playing music with his brothers, avoiding Honolulu crowds.

Like many Hawaiians, Dante's family name was English, in their case, the Wellingtons from the green hills of Waimea on the Big Island and, generations later, the dry red hills of Aiea on Oʻahu. Local people thought that the Hawaiians who lost their Hawaiian family names were linked with those British and American explorers and missionaries who intermarried for title to land. If this were so, then the Hawaiians who lost their family names were probably royalty, the ones who held the mighty ahupuaʻa, divisions of land from the top of a mountain range down to the coast, an ancient way to ensure that each part contained the whole—mountain watershed, cultivated plateaus, and sandy coasts with good fishing.

No one talked about the daughter of a missionary, maybe a Miss Mary Wellington, who was betrothed to a dark-skinned Hawaiian whose family descended from a war lord with absolute and terrible power. Silver gelatin photographs of Miss Mary captured the heart shape of her face as well as the white folds of her long dress, fine handkerchief cotton limply outlining her soft plump shoulders. Some time after the formal joining of two families, there was a long afternoon of sequestered love, the brooch at her throat was unfastened, her skirts lifted, a child conceived. Quill pens dipped into a pot of ink, signatures were scratched on deeds of land and trust.

For a warrior line, there is no such thing as dilution of blood. The Wellingtons were Hawaiian with an English name: looking at Dante and his family, no one would mistake them for anything but native Hawaiian. When a noble falls from great heights, he wears a mask of servitude, sometimes as a day laborer who drives a truck or digs a trench for a house foundation, sometimes as a drunken clown who steals just enough to drink again. Not all workers and clowns are noble. The ones who are noble, fallen from grace, command a wider swath of a street or sidewalk: they do their job, seething with another purpose just beneath the mask. The others take smaller steps and less space: wearing no mask, no disguise to allow one person to bow down, serving two purposes, one true and the other false.

To see the true person and his disguise at the same time calls for two pairs of eyes, looking outward at the world and inward at oneself. Not everyone recognized Dante as a fallen noble. The ones who knew of his true identity were like Gloria, the ones who were waiting for something to happen, any day, keeping a remnant of memory from diminishing into nothing. Looking at a man such as Dante made it possible for others, the observers, to accept the proposition of day and night:

we can see the crisp edges of labor and profit in daylight; we fall asleep at night, knowing how unprotected we are from those things that defy shape and color. Looking at Dante is like mistaking day for night, a young warrior walking, an old ghost not far behind.

Many of the women in Kailua noticed Dante. Like Gloria, many had waited for their assigned rubbish day to catch a glimpse of the big man jogging next to the truck. A few had spent what seemed like their entire adult lives waiting for him to appear, loving and renouncing him, surprised by a wiry goatee and then reassured weeks later by his clean-shaven face. Part of the intrigue was his wordlessness: the women of the town had no idea what he liked to eat (though each thought she had a good idea), what he liked to do (aside from playing music), what he wanted out of life (he didn't seem like the marrying kind). Mrs. Makahoehoe said that he was married once before right out of high school. Mrs. Yamaguchi said that he had a long-time girlfriend who was beautiful but had a hot temper—she would throw furniture at him, walk out, then come back. Someone else said he was a loner, grieving for his younger brother who died in the war. Gloria thought he was the moody type, given to long silences and suppressed rage, inclinations that made him a looming dark figure in her mind, an absence with physical dimensions. She was glad to carry such a burden, it kept her from detaching and floating into thin air.

Pushing through the back door, it was all she could do to set down the groceries on the kitchen counter. With weak arms, she remembered to put Ezra's chocolate milk in the icebox. Everything else would have to wait. Lying down, holding a square cushion to her chest, she took a long nap.

When the twins came home from school they changed into play clothes and ran outside. They collected violet-red bougainvillea petals in their old Easter baskets. When the baskets were full, they knelt beside the driveway, in a shady spot near the house, pounding the petals with rocks. While Lana continued to beat the thin veined petals, her sister Liz ran to the corner of the house, pulling the green garden hose over to the driveway. Then she ran into the house to get two empty glass jars and long cooking chopsticks. She did everything her older sister told her to do. Together they mixed bruised petals and water to make red colored water.

"I'm the mother and you're the baby," Lana said. Her sister's face relaxed into a smooth blank zero. Inside the zero was another one, a small O-mouth.

"It's a long winter and there's no food in the village. Everybody has died." Liz is respectful, watching her sister's face grow stern with hardship.

"Here, take this, it's bitter medicine." Liz obediently pretended to drink the colored water, making baby glugging noises.

The girls continued to pretend aloud, talking and making more colored water, their voices sifting through the screen next to the living room sofa where their auntie napped. The suspension of taking a daytime nap combined with girls' voices just outside the window tethered the sleeper to the surface: just above were the sharp edges of things she would recognize, below were the changing shapes distorted by exhaustion, like the torpor of Sleeping Beauty before she was found by the prince. Walking through the silent courtyard of suspended animation, the garden fallen into brambly thickets, the prince was probably hiding his unease from his hunting consorts—what unseen hand has wrought this effect? Why me, why not the rogue prince across the river who gets drunk with shepherds and sleeps in the open fields? He is rough and stupid enough not to be bothered by a hundred-year sleep. There are royals who went down in history wishing hard that no miracles would ever happen on their watch. With dragging steps, the prince ascended the staircase to the tower. He was young, inexperienced, filled with dread. It was easier to draw a heavy bow and kill a deer, watching his men wield their knives to dress the animal, tie its legs to a litter. Thinking better of it, the prince turned around and left the scene. Let the rogue prince discover the sleeping girl.

Gloria got up from her nap, forgetting whatever she had dreamed, struck by the lateness of the day. She heard her sister in the kitchen, putting away the fresh groceries she had left to wilt in the heat. Although her sister cooked the family dinner, she always consulted with their mother before she started. The old woman would smack her lips, suggesting something impossible like roast duck and steamed buns; then her daughter would say, how about corned beef patties, and the old woman would say, that's good too. This familiar exchange gave Gloria a terrific itch: she wanted to slap her old mother into realizing that her sister was not such an agreeable daughter, it just appeared that way. Really, her sister was the b-o-s-s of the h-o-u-s-e.

Over the years, the house on Keaniani Lane filled with more people, including the lingering presence of those who had left for elsewhere. The dead seemed to occupy the most space of all (immovable boulders) because they would appear in one spot and stay there, not participating in the random movement of the living.

Out of a sense of modesty the adults in the house tended to avoid the center of a room (that would call too much attention to oneself). Only children would think of a room as a circle and the center as their place to set up a game of milk bottle tops, stacking them and throwing one down with a snap (whatever toppled over were theirs), then forming new stacks (the winner with the ziggurat of cardboard tops would soon be the loser), standing, falling down. The dead occupied the center of rooms, the center top step outside the kitchen door, vantage points for those who no longer have a separate will, no volition to do anything but sit for long periods of time. When the girls sat on the top step with their chins propped on the heels of their hands, elbows balanced on their raised knees, they both benefited from the advice of their dead doubles, cousins who played in tents near the fields. Faint voices reminded the twins that things were not so bad after all, as long as they could get up and go outside to play, as long as they had one another. Of all the rooms, the dead preferred the front room with the television (as a large common space, it was vacated more than occupied; its center could hold more than one boulder of the dead). Small and quick, the children could slip around them without interrupting their games. When Mother needed to sit and think she sat in a straight-backed chair in the kitchen, against a wall, under Father's calendar of high and low tides.

When we die we tend to stay with those close to us, occupying our houses as wordlessly as a table or chair. We listen, have opinions, find out a few surprising things about our children or grandchildren, how swift and mean it gets between them. Great Auntie Agnes covered her eyes when one child pinched or scratched another. If she were alive, she would hold the crying child. Then she would pop a hard candy into the child's mouth. The child would look at her with serious eyes, absorbed in the taste of something sweet, cracking the shell with his molars, flattening the jelly center against the roof of his mouth. Auntie Agnes kept a tall glass jar full of hard striped candies with jelly centers like money in the bank.

With time on our hands we can sit and watch the world go by. When Rene dreams, he is caught in the rat run of a young man who wants to sing into a microphone; when Mother dreams, she's spoiling a grandchild, living in her son's house; when Ezra dreams, he is with the strangers inside the television, dashing around town in a new car. The dead never get tired of sitting in one place; without a will separating them from others, they can take it easy, humming familiar tunes.

As long as we feel the pressure and weight of things, we will want something we do not have, something thick and sweet. Given the thinnest wedge of possibility, we break out in a sweat from our efforts to obtain what we want.

✺

There seemed to be less space and fewer hours in the day, wearing out Gloria's routine for peace and quiet. She wanted to keep the game going but was running out of cards, nowhere to go, to sit down and think. As a child she liked to play solitaire, flipping over one card after another. Grown up, each day felt like a flipping card; the thought of life as a game of chance frightened her, the sense that mere chance could change everything. As an antidote to fear, she developed a voiceless narration that could countermand any game of cards.

Whenever Gloria felt her trance talk coming on, she worried that someone would catch her at it. They would think she was talking the way the twins do when they pretend starvation or fame. But Gloria's trance was not a game and the story of it could not be changed at will. Moving her lips silently felt like reading a book, automatically reading her own story according to the gurgles of air within, bubbles pushing upward, congesting her throat. All she could do was click her tongue, occasionally lick her lips when the story went on and on like an unraveling shawl. But once she succumbed to the trance, falling into the middle of the story, there was nothing she could do to stop it.

Dante always approached from a distance, striding toward her as if he had walked a long way, across a hard flat desert, one foot in front of the other, the kind of walking that strips a man down to himself. The thought of all those years of waiting coming to an end was almost unbearable: patience had become part of her, the way in which she inhabited the world. The longer she waited, the greater the possibility. Soon all of this would come crashing down on her, at any moment he would be on her doorstep, standing in front of her. That was the difficult part, reminding herself to breathe, to look at him.

Clicks of the tongue accompanied her moving lips as she recited in a calm and silent voice the language of longing, those things that move underground, leading a life as secret as the shiny black beetle that burrows as we sleep. Dante hesitates as he reaches the bottom step of the porch, his foot stops there and he leans forward. She offers him a glass of water, moving her lips, extending her arm. No, that's all right he says. All right then, she says.

She looks at him: he doesn't seem to mind, looking away at the drooping fruit trees in the yard, down at her small bare feet. She is saying something. It's just as well we didn't meet sooner, that would have been too soon. He is looking away but his head is inclined as if listening closely. She continues, for many years I was foolish enough to expect what nobody else I know ever got, what they call the American Dream. Before the war nobody talked like that because those same people were just little children. We didn't know any better, playing in the sand, digging and molding cakes and pies. I don't really dream about us in a house on a street (this remark amuses him)—that would be too much like my sister. We could be happy on the beach (this really hits his funny bone) like the Hawaiians who live on the beach most of the year and disappear when it rains. When it rains we can move temporarily to a restaurant, an out of the way place with a table and two chairs (this arrangement does not strike a chord with him, they leave the scene quickly). We are meant to wander around, holding hands, looking at every little thing. (He thinks of the things he loves, ice water and salty air.) If you asked me to marry you I would say why not and we wouldn't have to wait a minute longer. We would be married at the same time we both agreed to it and everybody would find out later. I would tell everybody about us and (I hope) you would too. (Dante doesn't seem to mind this part of the story. Persuasion is music to his ears, just another song.) That's it. We'd be together, holding hands, walking around, waving to everybody. Then we could sit on the beach, looking at the water. At night, we would be husband and wife— you'd be surprised how intuition works wonders and you would surprise me because a man like you can be slow to give up himself. (This is the last straw! Gloria's story has brought the big man down. He is laughing; his face is streaked with tears of joy.)

That's the other nice thing about waiting, clearing the air. Waiting, one gets tired of most things, finding them unnecessary. It's amazing how many things I can live without—a husband? house? and, of course, there's no need for any of the things in my cedar chest, not even the fluffy white towels. I probably don't even need you! (Why does that make you smile?) But I know in my heart that if, and that's a big if, if I could have you the whole world would change. Why? I'm not sure. Maybe I'd stop worrying about getting old. We could walk on the beach, holding hands. You could make me laugh. I could remind you of something you'd have forgotten. You could sing, not to me but to the open air, your voice not so big and loud, carried off in gusts of ocean air. The more I think about it, the more it seems to be so. (Moving her lips, clicking her tongue.) Maybe this is what love is, waiting so long that almost nothing matters. All the little things fly away.

Looking is loving: I could look at you all day long. Gloria extends both arms, embracing a space about the size of Dante. Your skin is sticky with the heat. There must be days when it is unbearable, the hot sun making you thirsty and sweaty. Those are the good days, when all we want is a sip of water, to sit down. Come here, let's sit together, you can sit first and I'll squeeze in between you and the wall. There's time, maybe tomorrow, to walk on the beach. We have all the time in the world! (Clicking her tongue, she settles on the top step. She looks all around her, at the low hedge and patches of yellow grass. Sitting, she draws her legs and arms together, pressing her face against the outside wall of the house.)

That night Ezra sat at the table wearing his coonskin cap with its striped tail, drinking chocolate milk, his rifle trailing a cork and string from its long nozzle. Uncle Shorty read aloud from the *Honolulu Star-Bulletin*,

> Norman Vincent Peale arrived today on the *S.S. Lurline,* greeted by delegations from Honolulu churches and schools. Reverend Peale will conduct open-air services on the grounds of Queen Emma's summer palace on Sunday, June 2, 1952.

Unlike Gloria, Shorty did not believe in the power of positive thinking. He felt sorry for his sister whenever she quoted Reverend Peale's rules for improvement based on scientific research. He thought the Reverend Peale's television sermons were the same as the commercial breaks for Ipana toothpaste, "Brush-a,

Lurline in town.

brush-a, brush-a / with your new Ipana," a voodoo jingle for a voodoo priest.

Gloria asked Shorty to drive her to the service. He said of course but Eunice might come along. Gloria nodded. Shorty felt apologetic, knowing how much his sister and girlfriend disliked each other. He shook the paper and continued reading in a television voice,

> A traveling businessman on the *Lurline* said that Reverend Peale conducted services onboard and went out of his way to get to know his fellow passengers. "He taught us the difference between an ear full of trouble and a mind full of peace. I was hounded by worry, doubting my ability to close the biggest deal of my life, and now I feel confident, ready to face the world."

It was a front-page story with a photograph of the Reverend Peale wearing flower lei piled up to his ears. Another delegation was waiting for him at the Royal Hawaiian Hotel where he would be staying. Throughout the week, tourists gathered on the sandy beach below his balcony, waiting for him to step out and wave both arms, reaching out to his people.

Edward Afong, Dan Poepoe, and Eddie Kinilau.

Why This Boy

By noon it was pau hana for the rubbish crew. Returning to the city and county lot, they parked the big rumbling truck and had a few beers together, leaning against the curves of the high cab, reaching in for another cold bottle. Not only was it pau hana for the day but also for the week, high Friday before a Saturday first birthday and a Sunday wedding, a busy music weekend for Dante and his brother Moses. Both brothers had good steady jobs but they agreed that Dante had the better situation, a rubbish man on a winning crew who started before dawn and finished by noon. Moses worked construction, getting off when it rained. The best rubbish crews stayed together for years, eventually getting the better residential routes whose household rubbish accumulated according to habit and did not exceed the limits of one large rubbish can.

Dante's crew consisted of a driver and two runners. As one of the runners, Dante jogged beside the truck and maintained a rhythm of upending and tossing cans without a break so that the truck never came to a dead stop. That was the trick. The runners worked both sides of the street, hopping onto the back whenever that street was pau, as the truck picked up speed over to the next leg of the route. According to tradition, rubbish routes were managed as piece work, meaning there were no required hours to put in, just a route to complete according to the day of the week. Starter crews were assigned commercial routes that were slow and backbreaking. Between the town traffic and the density of discard materials of hotels and restaurants, it was almost impossible to keep a rubbish truck going without stalling between too many people and cars. Old-time crews got the nice routes in outlying areas where streets were dotted with neatly kept houses and small children waved as if a rubbish truck were a chariot bearing young warriors and the spoils of war. People felt apologetic about their excess rubbish, especially bulky items that should go straight to the city dump. They waved with long faces, pointing to their nuisance rubbish, holding up their hands as if to say, "Forgive us, we are well aware of how unreasonable our rubbish can be, especially when we bother to clean out the garage, lucky thing we'll never bother to clean out the really serious clutter in the back yard, lucky for you, rubbish guys!"

Over the days before Christmas, Dante's crew scooped up cases of beer and red envelopes of twenty-dollar bills along their routes, tangible apologies for all of the embarrassing free loads of non-regulation rubbish left at the edges of people's grassy front yards. One young mother stood by her contribution of beer and cash early in the morning, guarding it against the neighborhood bad boys, holding her fat baby who pulled at her breasts. The young woman smiled sweetly and radiantly at Dante, not afraid to meet his eyes.

Before the sun came up, in the mauve hours of early morning, a rubbish man could observe many interesting things. Who was that woman holding her slippers to her chest? The man who silently rolled his car down the street? Not Romeo and Juliet, they were more like the Nurse and Friar getting a second chance in a small town, old friends in the light of day, but under cover of night, strangers who asked so many questions of one another, those things we find telling or piquant. On those early mornings, waiting for the sound of tires on gravel, she wore something unfamiliar, a white robe tied with a sash, the slippery satin flowing down to the floor. He carried in a chocolate mayonnaise cake, set squarely in a cardboard box, and took the empty box home with him when it was time to go. A large dog watched the Nurse and Friar as well as the rubbish men, opening his mouth so wide that his eyes shut tight in reflex. The crew called that one the talking dog, opening and closing his mouth without a bark.

The rubbish men laughed about these early morning sights over their pau hana beer. Not Dante. He found such fleeting moments almost too wonderful to bear, like an onshore wind that delivers the smell of wide water and salt on the skin. The vision of a young woman with uncombed hair, holding a baby, was too great a burden for such a fierce man who was no longer as young or as full of possibilities as the young woman. Somewhere in his grown man's mind, he wanted to be that baby in her arms, pressing his face to her breast, wanting milk and the warmth of her skin. He wanted to fall asleep in her arms, holding onto that sweet sleep of a baby who has nothing better to do than cling to his mother's warmth, drawing in her scent, curling his toes, pushing against her body.

When Dante was a young boy following his mother around, she would praise him by saying, "Why this boy," meaning why this particular boy, why this boy who follows so closely in his mother's footsteps, listening first to her breath, then to her conversation and songs, those mele that carry a melody like waves on the water but hint at a hidden meaning, the rocking motion of a man and woman sharing a bed. At a young age, he could imitate the lilt of his mother's voice, preferring to

Refuse pick up.

Hawai'i soldiers in Korea.

Black Hair,
White Wings

readfruit hung from the tree, yellow-green spiky
balls attached by curving stems. Grandmother
carried a white enamel basin filled with dishwater
to splash around the tree. It was wasteful to throw
away water. On the plantation where she raised her
family, everyone carried dishwater to their patches of
vegetables. Wives did the washing and husbands did
the drinking and gambling.

Her first husband had taken the long steamer trip
from Korea to the Hawaiian Islands thinking that he
could get work grooming horses. He had heard that the
plantation owners maintained stables for their pleasure
and would appreciate a charming man who could walk
horses around the grounds, warming them up for their
riders who would call them by name, "Long Black Hair"
or "White Wings."

When he arrived in the islands, people laughed at this idea, laughing longer and louder when they learned that he knew nothing about horses. He told them about the horses looking for a good pair of hands to brush them down, lead them across the green grass, wave to the birds in the trees. People roared at this remark, slapping his shoulders too hard, as if they were thick horse flanks. Smiling too much while he worked in the fields, he despised anyone who was just like him, a poor immigrant who ran up debts, unable to get ahead.

When he left and never came back, Grandmother cried for days. She covered her head with shame and stayed in the house. Then she carried her baby girl next door to a neighbor, asking her to take the baby so that she could look for work. Nodding with a long face, the neighbor gathered up little Gloria into her arms and propped her next to her baby boy. When she fed the boy, she fed Gloria; the babies grew up doing and getting the same. In those days, people took in other people's children without asking too many questions. Hānai, adoption without papers, provided a way to escape a dead end, subverting one's lot in life, payment deferred and then forgotten.

Grandmother could not find work so she opened a lunch spot on the edge of the field. She cooked in the open, good hot food in a big pot on the hibachi. Other women disapproved, but she continued to cook, even in the rain, throwing up a slanting tarp to keep the fire from going out. It was a comfort to eat a bowl of hot rice and sip tea over lunch. Soon the men found it preferable to spend a few coins for lunch, gathering around for stories, than to lug around a cold pail of leftovers.

She met her second husband in the field, a man who would never dream of horses. Even after they married, she kept up the lunch business, attached to life at the edge of the fields.

Gloria grew up thinking the neighbor was her mother and the boy was her brother. After she realized which woman actually bore her, it was too late to change her habit of thought, so she called both of them mother. When her real mother gave birth to two boys, one after another, she took Gloria back, relieving the neighbor of another mouth to feed. Gloria took in the boys as if they were strangers instead of half-brothers, imitating the sad smile of her neighbor mother. Whenever she missed her neighbor mother more than she could bear, Gloria took the boys next door for tea and cookies. The boys tugged at her flat girlish breasts and tired her out. When they grew big enough to run around, they forgot all that she had done for them, leaving her stuck in the house. The boys yelled at their older sister and at each other, a rising, hollering sound of wild joy, running off to play in the muddy ditches with the other boys.

Born last, Mother grew up thinking Gloria was her mother because she was so much older, always complaining about the boys. By then, people were leaving the plantation for town. The neighbor lady who raised Gloria stayed behind, not willing to move from the camp for the luxuries of running water and electricity.

Years later, Grandmother heard that the neighbor lady lost everything and moved into the plantation owner's house. She raised several generations of haole children and lived a long life. When she died, she was mourned by her adopted family. They buried her on the plantation, under a big drooping hau tree, its narrow green leaves dipping in the breeze. Many years later, a young girl sat under that tree, holding a book and listening to swishing leaves all around her. The girl had long, pale yellow hair loosely braided down her back. She missed her school friends on the mainland, wishing important jobs did not take her father to faraway islands in the middle of nowhere. Her mother was lonely too, worried about her daughter who no longer smiled, wondering how to make them both feel better, cheerful and ordinary. All day long, the girl sat under the tree.

Someone told Grandmother that her first husband did not return to Korea but showed up in bars around town. He told people that he was going to buy land on the Big Island and raise horses. As a married woman with two young boys, she made one visit to her first husband's grave. She spent her second husband's hard-earned money on oranges and a bottle of whiskey as a parting gift befitting a man who died in his prime. There was no stone marker, just a wooden cross that was already listing backward, as if in disbelief. She knelt down and piled the oranges in a neat pyramid. Then she poured the contents of the bottle onto the ground. Her little sons played on the grass between the rows of markers. The boys touched the various treats left on the graves, hard puckered oranges, round white manapua buns stuck to paper, red torch ginger in metal cans of water. She slapped the boys when they tried to sneak a treat for themselves. Eyes watering from the sharp uptake of whiskey fumes, she felt satisfied that the dead man knew she still loved him.

When Mother and Father moved into their married house it was the start of something new and promising. The house was painted white with a dark green trim, sitting squarely in its lot, distinguished by a pink concrete driveway. On a dead-end lane, the neighbors each had a clear view of one another. No one bothered to put up a fence. Father planted a mock orange hedge along the front of the yard, trimming it low so that the neighbors knew this was just for show, complementing the paint job on the house. Mother said it was just right: it was a dream house.

Over the years, the neighbors watched Father's various home improvements. First, he closed off the porch for Gloria's bedroom. Then he closed off the garage to add another room for Fatso and Shorty. The neat square house lost its sense of balance; it began to look like a big box with high windows. Everyone on the lane wondered, what's going on in there? The neighbors had difficulty keeping track of the family's comings and goings since there was no front screen door to open and bang shut: people seemed to magically disappear and appear at all hours of the day and night. Children on the lane repeated what they heard at the dinner table, that this was the funny kind house that looked different from all the rest. Neighborhood talk turned more pointed and curious about the funny kind people in the funny kind house. The wife must be the b-o-s-s if the house is stuffed with her relations.

The house absorbed the talk like a boulder holds the warmth of the sun. It was a vessel that wanted more wine. Its hot roof and shady eaves sang in the open air.

Hauling out bucket and ladder, Father painted the house different colors whenever it suited him. One year it was green and gold like a Christmas tree. Then red and yellow like a pagoda. This time, it was a sunny coral orange that could just as well be a vacation cabana on the Caribbean. Mother said this was the best yet. Gloria said nothing.

The other houses were properly maintained as model starter homes. When the neighbors entertained, their relatives brought gifts of food and drink, then they left to go home to their own houses somewhere else in town. This is what was supposed to happen, visitors coming and going. Father liked to say that if he charged rent he would be a rich man.

At dusk, the gaudy house took on a soft glow, through the dim light it seemed to vibrate slightly, a big soft boulder of time forgotten, when families lived closer together, sometimes with nothing more than a flap of rain tarp between one breathing body and the next. Plantation houses were not really houses as much as fortified tents and shacks. There was no virtue in the poverty of it but rather a sense of everyone being in the same boat. The lowest man on the totem pole was the stingy one, the one who hoarded his cash and liquor. Only a fool would put on airs of being better than his neighbor. It's a mean thing to laugh at a man who dreams of grooming horses instead of tilling the fields, but it's also only natural to laugh. What else can one do in the face of such a dream?

Ezra held the ladder steady for his father, one boy foot on the lower rung, unsmiling and proud of his afternoon job. The boy's head still had some of its infant proportion, too big for his body, a round dome in which his brain could grow without impediment. Descending the ladder, Father could see his son as the gods above might see him, a large, thoughtful head set on the narrow shoulders of a boy. When he looked at Ezra, he saw himself as he might have been, full of promise, different from all the rest. The set of the boy's head was unbending, his attention to his father was stalwart like a young soldier who has not seen war. He must be spared, Father thought, such an unyielding stance in one so young, stiff-necked, full of pride.

Thankfully, Ezra was far too young to be enlisted, the ground war in Korea predicted to end any day, as soon as U.S. troops could move the line further north, push back the commies streaming down from China, scaring smooth-faced soldiers with their crazy-ass bugles and whistles. The worst was when they yelled in the faces of the boys with nothing left but their bayonets. Pushing the line farther north, MacArthur would call up Deuce Four to precede the First Cavalry. Although the soldiers were taught to spare the peasants in their traditional white garb, the distinction was lost when confusion set in. The Chinese horns and whistles drove everybody nuts. Small children riding on the backs of their mothers, all dressed in dirty white cotton, looked just like humpbacked Chinese soldiers in dark uniforms, yelling spooky epithets. How the hell was a U.S. soldier supposed to tell the difference?

If the war dragged on and the boy went, he would have to live, eat and sleep in his U.S. uniform. With the face of both his ally and enemy, the rounded square Korean face, he would advance unprotected against the line. The only-surviving-son rule might keep him home, if his pride would let him stay put.

Father once told his bride that they would take a trip to Korea, see their homeland for the first time and bring back lavish gifts for the family. He had wanted to see the isolated rivers and valleys of the north, those places heavy with mist and cold, staying in a village inn with heated floors and heavy cotton blankets. He wanted to inhabit an ancestral world where he would reap admiration and respect over time, growing long white hair, wearing a tall horsehair hat with a wide brim. Instead, his sense of the distant past was reduced to hot spicy foods and a reputation for a corresponding bad temper. He hoped his son inherited his temper—it would protect him from the cowards who wanted to improve the world beyond recognition.

Father folded the ladder and set it against the house. Without saying a word, his own stubborn head jerked toward the lane, signaling that his son could run out and play. The boy ran, joining the other boys who were planning a late-afternoon mango raid on a big house with a six-foot fence on Oneawa Street. It would be difficult, but not impossible, to climb the fence without getting caught. They would knock green mangoes down with sticks, more than they could eat, just keep knocking them down, thrilled with the sick thud of fruit hitting the soft ground. Whoever brought back the most mangoes was the winner. At dusk, huddled in the driveway of the funny kind house, the boys would peel mangoes with pocket knives. Someone would bring the necessary supplies: they would dip the sour green fruit into a cup of soy sauce and vinegar, sprinkling each bite with black pepper, scrape their teeth on the hairy seed, hurling the seeds into a neighbor's yard. They would eat green mango in this way until their stomachs hurt and their teeth tingled. The afternoon raid would be sudden and relentless. They were ready.

That night was warm with no ocean breeze. The boys stayed out late in the driveway, laughing, pushing, farting green mangoes. Father listened to the boys, wishing he had a few friends to joke around with, young men in uniform who walked around in twos and threes, wondering what town they were stuck in. He had so many relatives that friends had seemed out of the question, but he missed what he didn't have now. Maybe he had been particularly foolish all these years, industriously painting the house various colors of the rainbow. Maybe he wasn't thought of as a contrary-minded philosopher, maybe his neighbors thought he was way too peculiar, someone not to be taken seriously.

After the war, nobody took him seriously, not even his wife. If Sam or Ipsy had survived and come home with him, they could go out drinking, enjoy the cool dark interior of a Honolulu bar. Like other local boys, they preferred the privileges of the uniform in place of their white T-shirts. In uniform they were not stopped for curfew, the state of martial law in the islands directed at males with a Japanese face.

On the isolated, northernmost island of Ni'ihau, the war was fought on different terms. Nobody there listened to the radio or watched television. Honolulu people thought that everyone on Ni'ihau was a little crazy, inbred over many generations. If not crazy, they were surely thought of as backward, a bunch of locals, mostly Hawaiians, living under the land ownership and largesse of the Robinson family. After the attack on Pearl Harbor, one Japanese pilot did not make it back to his carrier, unable to locate that floating dot in the Pacific. He landed in a dry, scrubby field on Niʻihau. A Hawaiian man took his boots and identification papers. Another Hawaiian went through the damaged plane and carried away the ammunition from the machine guns.

But a local resident named Yoshio Harada recognized the face of this pilot, the face of someone he had not met before, a sign that something important was going to happen. Shaking with excitement, he gave the pilot a shotgun, a small tribute to a nearly overwhelming vision: for the first time in his life, he had met someone who could have been him, speaking in Japanese and jabbing the air with his finger. Yoshio spoke only baby talk Japanese, but he nodded, looking at his mirror self with comprehension. Together they wrestled the machine guns off their mounts, only to discover there were no live shells.

The Hawaiians kept looking out for the Robinson sampan that carried weekly supplies from the island of Kauai, but the U.S. Army had forbidden the sampan from sailing. Desperate, the pilot burned down the house of the Hawaiian who would not return his papers. He confronted the man who had taken his ammunition with Yoshio's shotgun. Without his boots he looked like a scared boy. He fired three times into the big Hawaiian's stomach. The Hawaiian overpowered him and smashed his head against a stone wall. Yoshio leaned over the shotgun and pulled the trigger, falling next to the bloody head of the pilot. When the sampan finally returned, Robinson told his people that they had fought their own war. Benehakaka Kanahele, the man who took three shots in the stomach, survived and went back to his wife.

Of all the stories that were told, the one about the downed pilot on Ni'ihau was almost forgotten, an orphaned occurrence that only grew murkier and more ragged with time. There were no songs or stories about the short, fierce war that was waged on the island of Ni'ihau.

Whenever there was drinking and men of a certain age, war stories were told. The old stories were the best, how a young man almost dies of boredom, then almost dies advancing under fire, then dies and rises to heaven with a girl in his arms. With the onset of the Korean War so soon after the end of World War II, people's feelings about war, its moments of deprivation and glory, sunk into a tired muddle of changing alliances and embarrassing incidents. Returning soldiers said the Korean countryside was nothing but rubble and snow. The most pitiful stories were about mistaken identity, the problem of the wrong face and the right uniform.

❋

That night father got a bottle and drank. He could not patch together a reasonable picture of the future and he was too tired to think. He could not think of a single thing that could change the funny kind people in the funny kind house. He wished to start with a clean slate, a new wife and a new house. There were no colors in his dreams, just a deep black sleep. The next morning, Mother tried to shake him, with no effect. He slept all day, missing a day of work. He dreamed the house caught fire, filling with smoke, pushing out its occupants, no one he recognized. The blackened house fell in a heap, more people escaped, falling to the ground. When he got up the next day, he could see that nobody had died and the house had not fallen down. It was the same as ever.

Shorty offered to drive him to work.

"Nah, I'm all right. Feel like shit but I'm alive."

Father splashed water here and there, standing in front of the bathroom sink, taking a quick Filipino bath. He put on a white short-sleeved shirt, dark pants, and tight shoes, an outfit for his Japanese thoughts. He worked for the Territory of Hawai'i, comparing columns of figures for large-scale public works projects that had no beginning and no end. He missed the war and its large, colorful landscapes. He disliked his boss, a large freckled haole who combed his hair with his fingers whenever he took a piss in the men's room.

Shorty was standing in the driveway, waiting.

Feeling cold and slightly sweaty, Father got into the Packard. Shorty drove without saying a word, expertly climbing the Pali road without hitting the brake. Father rested the length of his arm on top of the front seat, a wide upholstered seat like a sofa. His brother-in-law's car was better than his. As the car descended into the valley road, the Ko'olau Range rose above low clouds. In every other deep green cleft, he could see a waterfall, the steep slopes were roaring with rain water, crashing down and blowing upward, a far off white spray. He nudged Shorty and pointed. They looked back to see the last of the upside-down waterfalls. The car took a wide curve and sped toward the city.

A Korean immigrant family.

Slippers
at the Door

In the great gyre that sweeps around the Pacific Ocean are lesser currents moving along similar orbits that are occasionally contradicted by swirls of thought puffing in a panic off earth tremors or sudden changes of temperature, casting a wide net of blue, plunging, swelling, lifting detached forests of rubbery kelp and miscellaneous lost cargo. Of all the things to wash ashore, by far the most commonly found are shoes, all kinds, from everywhere in the world—a curious fact considering how sinkable a shoe is, bound by a hard heel with a foot-sized cavity to hold watery sediment from the deep. For months, there was talk around the islands about the number of rubber-soled fishing shoes washing onshore. These were mismatched in size but all of a kind, Japanese fishermen's, the old-fashioned ones that lace up like women's booties. Where did they come from? No official report came in from Japan about a shipwreck or missing cargo.

The back steps of the house leading up to the kitchen door were piled with slippers, small dressy ones that belonged to Grandmother's funeral club. Members met monthly at someone's house, a nice way to rotate the work and to take a peek at one another's lives. Normally, the ladies snacked on sweet sticky pastries and tea, but Mother had prepared a regular lunch, apologetic that so many ladies had to be brought over from the Honolulu side by their grown sons. The ladies ate more than expected (there would be no leftovers), piling their plates with steaming rice and spicy Korean chicken, fried crisp then lightly tossed in a tangy sauce. A whiff of vinegar rising from a steaming platter whets the appetite.

Mrs. Kim talked the least, eating daintily but steadily. She was the leader of the Honolulu side who started the funeral club after her Japanese and Chinese church friends told her about the idea. This was the Korean club, smaller and less organized, charged with strong opinions from the start, primed for secret splinter groups. They ate first, then took roll call and collected the one dollar in monthly dues. Generally, the accumulation of time and money worked well: when a member died, all the other members attended the funeral service and the club bought a large wreath on wooden stilts with a satin sash that said "Korean Ladies Funeral Club" in Korean characters. It was a good idea and they wished that they had thought of it first, before the Japanese and Chinese.

After the money was counted twice and put away, Grandmother invited the twins into the living room to greet the ladies. The ladies oohed and aahed over the girls, admiring their clean bright faces. Lana whispered something to Mother and Mother conferred with Grandmother. Another good idea was born, the girls would perform, after a few minutes of preparation, for the ladies. First, they appeared in plastic straw-colored hula skirts and danced the Hukilau, singing the song that everybody in Hawai'i knew by heart. Then they changed back into their play clothes and put on their favorite record, the Bunny Hop, sung by Arthur Godfrey on the ukulele. Then, the Hokey Pokey.

As the girls were putting their left leg in and their left leg out, shaking it around and turning it about, the ladies grew restive in their chairs. Something like an itch, a quick sting, a bug in her ear, caused Mrs. Lee to get up. Standing behind her chair, she continued to watch the girls hop around.

In the circle of ladies, Mrs. Lee felt out of place, without her friend, the much younger Mrs. Lee. The younger one had been missing from the circle for the past year, having died in her sleep. Her husband woke up and found her splayed in an awkward position, as if reaching for a coconut high above her head, her fingers extended and stiff, pointing at the headboard of the bed. This was the girl he saw playing in a mission courtyard with other girls, the one he waited for until she was old enough to marry. He gave her an important funeral with catered Chinese food and a long row of open bottles of scotch: her funeral was bigger than their wedding because the girl he married had surprised even him, growing heavy and plump without a wife's aftertaste of regret: she looked the same as in her youth except that her face was full of knowledge, pink cheeks pushing up her teardrop eyes when she smiled. Every day of their life together, he read the Korean newspaper and his wife's face. He knew everything that happened in the Korean businesses and churches of Honolulu but his wife's face remained a mystery; when her eyes were full of tears she looked content, almost happy; when she smiled across the table, looking into his big-fisted man's heart, her eyes grew deep and sad, pulling away from his returning gaze.

The older Mrs. Lee and the husband of the younger Mrs. Lee had a lot in common, sharing the job of looking after the girl grown up, the duties of best friend and husband. Their children played together and the two mothers were always having tea at one another's house. The younger woman spoke freely of her husband's habits and preferences, referring to him as "old man." Everyone called him old man, an expression that contained the story of their first meeting and, now, their last. He was an old man who would bring home a paper sack of lichee nuts for his wife, peeling each one and popping it into her mouth.

The girls reprised their bunny hop, hopping out of the room then hopping back for the ladies' clapping. "Thassa way, thassa way!!" the ladies clapped and cheered. The girls covered their faces and ran away. Mrs. Kim rose from her place to resume the funeral club meeting, bringing up the neuralgic problem of which florist to patronize because of the clash between the Honolulu ladies and a club member's family business. A property owning widow, Mrs. Kim felt she knew better than the others, detesting troublemakers who wouldn't accept a final vote on anything.

Coming around to the center of the circle, Mrs. Lee surprised herself by interrupting Mrs. Kim, not by speaking out but by singing an old song:

> *Arirang, arirang, a-ra-ri-yo.*
> *Arirang ko-ke-ro no-mo-kan-da.*

Everyone knew the tune and words,

> *Walking over the peak at Arirang (you left me behind).*
> *You will be tired before you reach one mile.*

As she waved her arms, turning slowly to encourage the ladies to repeat the verse, Mrs. Lee felt young again, remembering the fat-cheeked smiles of her missing friend. Like the best songs in the world, the tune was simple with many verses. Even Mrs. Kim did not mind the interlude since she was the living repository of the most variations and verses; she was the leader, even in recalling long forgotten words. Mrs. Kim sang with conviction, punching the air, singing as if there were more verses than even she could actually remember. Feeling as light as a leaf, Mrs. Lee waved her arms as she sang. The older sang for the younger, her friend who seemed to smile for no particular reason, the careless look of a girl going to a party, her mother boo-hooing at the door.

From the kitchen, the girls watched the ladies get up from their seats, swaying their bodies to the upward wail and downward beat of *Arirang,* filling the room with their voices. Normally resistant to outsiders, the small crystal bowls of candy resting on white doilies took notice of the dancing ladies; the clutter in the room that normally defeated Father's sense of order seemed to endorse both themselves and the visitors, a rising swirl of evidence that this house was fully inhabited by the living and the dead. The old sofa felt like a tired, sweaty horse, clip clop, clip clop, carrying more than its share, six ladies sitting abreast with their shadow husbands who kept their white shirts and dark coats on in the warm room, refusing to sing and relax.

The ladies called to the girls, requesting a second encore of the bunny hop. Liz followed Lana into the living room, waiting for her sister to strike their sassy opening pose, two bunnies who could hop with pizzazz. Even the more formal ladies who wore flesh-colored stockings up to their knees were tapping their feet, smoothing their skirts over their happy knees. The afternoon was a hit. The girls played more records, "She's Too Fat for Me" and "Just Five Minutes More" as Mother cleared the table.

When the grown sons returned to pick up their mothers, they poked their heads in, thanking Mother and Grandmother over and over again. Standing at the door, her feet in puffy pink bedroom slippers, Grandmother frowned in complete satisfaction, an empress dowager in stiff folds of red and gold.

The parade of sons was fascinating to the girls: they memorized them and discussed them later when they took a bath. They stayed in the bath and whispered until they were hoarse. They both liked the same one, Alphonse. He winked at the girls as if they were already eligible for his attention, everyone else in the house being ineligible, out of the question. Lana said he was probably engaged, who would let a fish like that get away? Liz said that sounded like something Auntie Gloria would say. Then they argued until the bath water turned cold. Shivering, they ran to the bedroom and put on their flannel nightgowns. They wore these until they got too warm, then they changed back into their play clothes.

That night after dinner, the twins were too excited to go to sleep. While the family slept, they talked speeded-up pig Latin and made rubber pancakes. After a while they switched from pig Latin's "fey, fey, fey" to their own French that sounded like "fou, fou, fou." Lana pretended she was a hotel chef in Waikiki. She instructed the audience, her sister, on the art of making the world's thinnest rubber pancakes: "Mix water and flour, melt butter in a pan, pour in one tablespoon of batter and slide it around. Count to one hundred. Flip. (The chef pursed her lips, releasing a puff of breath as the pancake landed with a sizzle.) After the edges turn crispy, put it on a plate...Pla-a-te!" the older girl repeated with a stern look. Gasping, the younger quickly handed her a plate (their favorite, a blue willow pattern), dipping an apologetic curtsy. "Sprinkle with sugar, roll tightly, mm-mmm!" Lana's hoarse whispers sounded desperately French: if she wore a starched toque it would be shaking like the top branches of a slender unfruited tree.

A head taller, the older one had an inner eye that could capture a dream: she was peering into a shop window filled with sweets; the one she wanted was three-tiered, laden with silver bullets and flowing ribbons shocked in mid-air, the impossibility of spun sugar. The younger face tilted upward, watching the older, more experienced face seize with joy, then settle into a look of sadness. Late into the night the girls whispered, their heads almost touching, as they bent over their mother's black cast iron pan.

Downtown Honolulu.

Going to Honolulu

The girls were begging Uncle Shorty to go to Honolulu. It was a hot Sunday and nobody was in the mood to take them to church. They loved church. Liz was always the fatally ill novice, the favorite of the old nuns. A weak imprint of a girl, born too soon after her sister, Liz looked sad and doomed for an untimely end; her narrow face could fill with sunlight ("let light perpetual shine upon them") or fall with shame ("in that day of trembling").

Lana was sick and tired of their precision coloring. She had invented a way to fill in color using small, even strokes with a sharp colored pencil; her sister copied her and together they had almost finished identical ballet coloring books. They worked in tandem, flipping through the pages, admiring their past work, agreeing on the next picture they would color side by side, the fatty mound below their thumbs rubbing the page as they worked. Everything was the same; only the twins could tell their work apart. The ballerinas in the pictures had fainting faces, their arms dripping white fingers, long-waisted torsos drooping light pink tulle, felled by the same heat and humidity that enervated the girls.

The twins thought of Honolulu as their grown-up life, a place to find their sweethearts. They wanted to walk around town, look into store windows, pretending they were on vacation from New York City. They shared an air-conditioned skyscraper apartment, working as office secretaries with black-framed glasses and straight skirts, dreaming of palm trees. (Lana was the kind of secretary men couldn't live without, taking off and putting on her glasses, listening to her boss's troubles, money owed, love lost.) Their big city girlfriends warned them about Hawaiian beach boys, but, as Lana would say, "When on vacation, anything goes."

Last year's birthday party for their great, great auntie Violet (even smaller and more wrinkled than Grandmother) was the last time they had been to town. They had worn stiff crinolines under their dresses and only saw the parking lot and interior of the Wisteria. It was a sit-down luncheon with Rene at the mike. Although it was unusual to let a young man MC the occasion, everyone agreed that he was a natural, someone who could speak intimately into a microphone. Rene's dream was to be an entertainer in a Honolulu nightclub. Thin and pale, he talked with his hands, touching his wavy hair. He inhabited his body like an actor, his sweet, soft voice rising from a dark hollow, reaching the ladies across the room, reminding them of times gone by. Mother loved Rene, a lost boy who took nothing from her, giving her long mournful looks in passing, like a bloom that fades.

For the birthday lunch, he wore a silky shirt and white pants, introducing the birthday girl, telling stories about her past sweethearts. Since he was too young to know her past, he made it up as he went along, suggesting that she almost married a famous local singer. She said she wondered how Rene knew so much. The pale young man just smiled and then dedicated a song to her, "Sweet Leilani, Heavenly Flower." Everyone drank a shot of Canadian Club between each course, toasting the birthday girl.

Gloria was taking her time dressing for Reverend Peale in Honolulu. The twins fixed begging eyes on Shorty.

"Please, please, we'll wash your car every day."

"Then wash the chamois and the sponges."

"Then the bucket!"

The girls dropped to their knees on the driveway, prostrating themselves before their uncle's black Packard. The sloping back of the car seemed to bend sympathetically toward the girls. It was a touchy moment, waiting for Gloria to come out and hoping Eunice would be ready when they picked her up. (The rival ladies would wear strikingly similar dresses, Gloria's in navy and white, Eunice's in red candy stripes.) It was out of the question to take the girls. Shorty knew that his sister did not want her daughters to grow accustomed to Honolulu sights, especially the boys in uniform and the tourists. Soldiers and tourists spelled trouble, that's why the kids in town grew up faster, aware of the haole who always had forward thoughts. Mother said that parading around in swimsuits and stretching out on the sand were exercises manufactured on the mainland and imported to the islands. She did not want her girls parading around; she wanted them in the house. Shorty often wondered if Eunice would jump for a haole, someone who bragged about business investments, someone tall and beefy and loud.

In the end, the girls were left behind. Shorty drove smoothly with his left hand on the wheel, the other resting along the top of the front seat. Gloria sat in the front seat until her place would be usurped by Eunice. The car ascended the Pali road at a leisurely rate, slowing around each curve, picking up speed, then slowing again. Although it was only twelve miles as the crow flies, the winding Pali road to Honolulu felt like a long journey through the mists of Shangri-la. When

Hotel Street.

Pali Road.

he drove alone, Shorty took the curves more quickly, tempting fate to fling him in his black car far out to sea, forever to be mourned by Eunice.

Norman Vincent Peale's public service was well attended. Official delegations sat in sections bounded by different colored ribbons. Shorty ushered the girls toward the front, off to the side in a shady spot, standing behind them. In another half hour the lawn was a sea of people, sitting in the noonday sun.

The speaker was introduced by a string of local officials including the mayor. The Reverend seemed to be hurrying through his sermon, uncomfortable in the heat but waving aside a proffered golf umbrella. He praised the blue sky and full attendance, prefacing his many praises with "only in Hawai'i." He explained how to break the worry habit and gave a prescription for heartache. Gloria didn't care for his prescription, it sounded like heavy housecleaning to chase the blues away. Why did he recommend long country walks for the boys and washing floors for girls? Eunice annoyed her by smiling even when bowed in prayer.

The service ended with a long "A-men," an easy chord struck by many voices. As the guest speaker and officials shook hands and filed off the platform, the organist abandoned her smile, her long, bony fingers running madly along narrow passages, a feverish, overwrought toccata, her last flourish sliding into a minor key, the foot pedals deepening the notes, the smothered caw-caw of doubt and sorrow.

Shorty steered the girls back to the hot car. He could hardly wait to deposit each one at home and then find Fatso. Together, the brothers would down a few cold beers, crunching on cold boiled peanuts, each bite tasting faintly of anise. One black star anise in a stock pot of boiling water goes a long way.

Early in the morning before the trade winds picked up, Father had left for Waimanalo pier. An impromptu gone fishin' day, he had not dropped any bread bombs the day before. All he had with him was a pole and a few slices of Love's bread that he pinched and shaped on the hook for bait. The condemned pier was no man's land, a place to sit and think. Holding the pole away from him, he jumped down to a solid-looking strut. Once he comfortably straddled the perch of white cracking wood, all he could see was water and sky. The morning light on the Waimanalo side is softer, endlessly gray until late morning. Father had a theory about morning light—the folds of gray and white that ran across the bay like a shower curtain, its motion playful, hiding something. When the day heated up, it fell like an iron sheath across the waters; behind the protective scrim of early morning was a hidden light; the light was hidden because if it were ever allowed to shine uncovered, it would kill him. The sun at midday is terrible, lacking glory, hot and flattening, so that things look like broken concrete instead of blue-veined marble, the soft shapes cast by light earlier and later in the day.

Father released the line with a whine from the reel, stopping the spinning with his thumb as the red puff ball hovered inches above the water. Any telltale dip of the puff indicated that a girl was nibbling at the other end. Mullet can nibble without getting their prim mouths caught on the hook, the most sensitive fish anywhere on earth.

Sophia's lips parted easily, for a sweet something, a sip of wine, a kiss.

He found Italian women a joy to behold: they laughed fearlessly, showing their teeth and pink gums. In Sophia's apartment, he was served tiny crystal glasses of wine, one after another. Feeling good, he told them stories about the islands, painting a picture of a golden sun, white sands, and endless, dropping blue. Sophia translated his stories into Italian; the old folks howled with glee—what's so funny about a warm, golden sun, he wondered. Sophia shared the two-room apartment with her parents, grandmother, two older women (who were sisters but not related to Sophia's family), and their four awful children, two predator and two prey to serious games of hide and seek. Sophia served him a slice of bread on a large plate. He brought gifts, cigarettes, canned meat, and U.S. dollars. She had a beautiful head of dark hair that fell into his face as she bent over him, smelling of oil and perfume.

The red puff ball bobbing breathlessly, Father pulled up a silver girl. (The scrim thrown over the hidden light had almost dissolved.) One more and he would call it a day. His wife could fry two of them crisp and salty. The men would sit in the patio, drinking and smoking, picking at the tasty fish with chopsticks. Not a complete meal, just an appetizer and small talk.

The following week, Shorty took Grandmother to the River Street fish market. The girls pleaded to go on the Honolulu errand. Mother said no. Gloria bowed her head in sympathy for the girls. Shorty pushed Grandmother into the front seat, a child-sized figure looking back at the girls. All day, he accompanied his mother to each market stall, carrying her bags of Chinese long beans and sweet red pork. Complaining about the prices, she bypassed the fish, shining and perfect in beds of crushed ice.

The girls were waiting in the driveway when they returned. It was a shame that they were not allowed to go with her, Grandmother said, but it was the right thing to do. She gave them each a folded packet of butcher paper containing multicolored popped rice. The twins ate one grain at a time, pretending they were poison pills.

That night Ezra came home after dark. Father rose from the table, glowering, until he saw his son's eyes filled with tears. He watched helplessly as his son pressed his wet face into Mother's soft breast. She held the boy's head against her until he stopped shaking with silent sobs.

The top of his right foot was scraped deeply, the skin jaggedly gone, showing pink flesh and pin pricks of blood rising and congealing at the surface. He had spent the day playing with boys at a construction site, running down dunes of gravel, rolling in cement dust, rocking backhoes from their parked positions. It had been a day full of honest work, hauling a pile of gravel from one side of the lot to the other, laughing madly at the confusion this would cause. They laughed so hard they cried real tears. Then they ran down the relocated gravel pile one last time. A big boy ran over him, like a Mack truck, grinding him into the small rocks. His face was nicked and red in spots, his foot chewed up, misshapen.

Ezra crept into the bathroom and called for his mother to follow. Only she could pick out the pieces from his raw foot, cleaning it carefully, swabbing the wound with hydrogen peroxide. In times of trouble, his mother acted swiftly with a hard heart.

Grandmother dropped everything she carried from the table to the kitchen sink. Almost all the dishes lay broken, leaking sauce, scattering bits of rice onto the yellow floor. Gloria, unaccustomed to kneeling, had to scrub hard to remove the food that the old pocked linoleum wanted to take in and digest. How could her sister put up with their mother's accidents? Every day? Her sister put up with a husband who didn't bother to talk to her and a mother who made a holy mess. At family parties, her sister would pat their mother and testify to her help in the kitchen, "Can't live without Mama, she can measure sugar and vinegar with the eye. She can make brown sauce by feel. When she was younger, she could make pie crust with her fingertips. Now I do that, but it was Mama who taught me." What a stupid lie. Their mother never made pies. They never had sweets as kids. Her sister lied about almost everything just to please their mother. Worse, she settled for marriage to Mr. Impossible, taking in more and more people, like a boat taking in water. Gloria was the only one, a delicate tick tocking instrument who knew what privacy and romance was all about.

Stuck with her sister's work, Gloria picked up the last bit of broken china and mopped the floor. There were only a few things left unbroken to wash and put away. Without realizing it, she was practicing the Reverend Peale's prescription for heartache.

Nu'uanu Pali.

School children at lunch.

Civil Alert

Ablack mynah bird squawked loudly, its yellow eyes drilling hungry holes through a green papaya stuck singly on the tree. Mother lifted and twisted off the fruit, taking it inside to ripen. The tree bore small sweet fruit, blooming and ripening one by one. It amazed everyone that the old bent tree continued to bear fruit, each one seemed like the last.

The end of school and the beginning of summer was just around the corner. Mother had dipped the twins' crinolines in blue starch water and hung them upside down on the clothesline, layers of stiff white stuck out like giant party flowers. Lana was completing sixth grade and moving on to intermediate school in the coming fall, leaving Liz behind for a long, lonely year. Although the girls would live through the next school year without expiring from loneliness, everyone in the family felt a little sad for them, especially for Liz who tended to be overly shy when she was not at home.

On the last day of school, Uncle Shorty was treating the family to dinner out at Princess Chop Suey, their favorite restaurant. It was a noisy place decorated with new Christmas ornaments draped over old, peeling ones—each year, a new layer of cheer added to the old faded faces of good luck and prosperity. Each person would pick a favorite dish, then Shorty would order a few more, then they would eat until they were stuffed and take the leftovers home in white boxes, evidence of his generosity stockpiled in the humming Frigidaire.

The girls dressed up for dinner out, pretending they were movie stars. They had to pretend quietly so that mother wouldn't disapprove. Gloria, watching the girls whisper and giggle throughout the many courses, felt a great sadness descend upon her shoulders. She remembered when she was a girl, constantly teased by her two brothers, on the brink of tears, her lips trembling. It was silly to feel left out of a children's game of pretend. She was losing heart, growing faint and small. She wanted to be part of a twosome, having dinner by candlelight, smiling mysteriously across the table. After dinner, Fatso and Shorty walked out arm in arm, flushed with food and drink.

Gloria rode in Shorty's car on the way back from the restaurant. She mistook the privileges of riding in the front seat with other privileges she did not have, asking too many questions about Eunice's intention to marry him. Given the softly whizzing air and the interior spaciousness of the Packard, almost a bedroom on wheels, Gloria's talk wandered, back to the restaurant and forward to a wedding, somebody's, in the family. She mentioned her willingness to find some really good Hawaiian music, authentic, low-key, maybe two brothers who harmonized and knew how to take requests; she would pay for it, a gift to Shorty and his bride.

At home, Gloria went to her room. Fatso, Shorty, and Father sat in the patio with cigarettes and cold bottles of beer. Father let Ezra swig from his bottle, the boy's mouth full of sour froth, grimacing like a man. The girls emptied their snap purses of their best hankies and the family's fortunes printed on slips of paper inside folded cookies. According to Father, Chinese business is good business: Every patron is promised luck and prosperity—in writing! That is the Chinese way. Koreans serve sticks of Double Mint gum and toothpicks after dinner, reminding their patrons that Korean food makes the mouth stink. That is the Korean way. After a Chinese dinner, we pat our stomachs, feeling rich, even our ears feel full of money. After Korean, our tongues on fire, we're ready for a fight, arguing over nothing.

Mother picked up Grandmother's broken dishes strewn all over the kitchen floor. As she kneeled down, the daughter told her old mother everything that happened at the restaurant—who they saw ("Remember Alphonse? Mrs. Lee's son? He was sitting close to a woman with two small children, not his"), what they ate ("too sweet, the sauces stretching the good stuff"), who paid ("Shorty gave a big tip, too"). Grandmother watched her daughter mop the floor: she was a good girl who told her mother everything.

The last time the girls were allowed into Gloria's room marked a dark narrow passage to becoming a woman, especially for Lana who was slowly pulling away from her sister even as her sister clung to her, registering her feelings only after looking at Lana's face, whether it was flaccid and sad or tightly convulsing with suppressed giggles. It was Liz' blank face, the presence of a child, that allowed Gloria to lapse into her trance talk with Dante. She blamed herself for his disappearance, letting three rubbish days go by without waiting at the window, sleeping while he worked, descending into her own fatigue over the devilish details of life. In the back of her mind she knew that no amount of voiceless talk would bring him back. Dante's appearance was not guaranteed like the promises of television. He did nothing attention-getting to recommend himself to the world, moving with the habit of someone who gets up early and sees the world before its bright waking hours. Gloria regarded the girls as the same small children she always cared for, learning to watch adult faces for clues about what's next, good or bad, the little girls who giggled endlessly when they were told to keep quiet.

Touching her brow, then the back of her neck, Gloria was moving her lips in full view of the twins. At first they didn't notice, too busy arranging the reds and pinks of nail polish in ascending order of intensity, the last called Fire & Ice, their auntie's favorite. Lana jabbed her sister and pointedly flashed her eyes at their auntie. The girls couldn't believe what they saw: they looked at each other and their disbelief instantly doubled; their auntie was moving her lips without sound, her eyebrows going up and down, her eyes growing hard then soft with tears. What was she doing? The girls kept still, afraid to break the spell, aware of the intrusion, as if they had walked into the bathroom and found their auntie naked. For a long while, the girls made themselves invisible, like black-garbed Noh players assisting their auntie's drama. Stealthily, Lana steered herself and her sister over to the cedar chest where they could huddle, allowing Gloria the length of the room to pace, roaming a vastly larger space between herself and the object of her love. Clicking her tongue, Gloria wandered the few steps back and forth along the length of her vanity between the bed and the wall with the sealed front door. The faintest utterance was on her lips, a whisper that seemed to call out a name. She touched her hair and seemed to answer, moving her lips, pausing, lips going again.

General Douglas MacArthur.

After that day, the girls no longer followed their auntie into her room to watch her brush her hair and pat her face with various treatments. And Gloria no longer expected the girls to follow her. In the middle of a story, Gloria understood that there were more days behind her than in front of her and she must hurry forward, running like a girl, toward the center of the dream. The dream was a changing dream with no beginning and no end. She no longer ruled her dreams, gladly giving up her pet ideas about love and marriage. Moving her lips, she spoke freely, without regret or a need for reply.

General Douglas MacArthur passed through Honolulu on a regular basis, on his way to Korea. He barely smiled, square-jawed and impenetrable behind dark aviator glasses. There was some hero talk but island people were still fatigued from World War II, especially the heavy presence of uniformed men in town and the whispered scandals involving soldiers and local girls. Everyone wanted things to return to the way they were before the mobilization of the Pacific theater, before everything new. The *Honolulu Star-Bulletin* carried headlines about "the 38th parallel." Pearl Harbor was both a memorial and an active naval shipyard. Like the arms race, the pace of change was speeding up, not slowing down. Each time the general passed through on military transport, there was a front page photo of him, laden with flower lei, lifting his arm in greeting, a leader's stern survey of crowds and ceremony.

In spite of the heat and humidity, nothing slowed down. School teachers nurtured their young sprouts as they had tended their victory gardens. Teachers believed that a combination of sun, water, and spelling would build sturdy bodies and minds. (The younger teachers dreamed of a love life after school; even a slight breeze at recess could set off alarming sensations beneath their light cotton dresses.) The twins obediently colored maps of the world—while every other place in the world was a color on a map, the children's reality was the island, the house in which they lived. Good weather seemed to cooperate with lesson plans that emphasized good habits and positive values. The girls learned about basic food groups and dental hygiene.

Even moments of anxiety seemed routinely scheduled. Once a month, civil defense sirens blared for a full minute at noon. Radios announced an alert at the same time, emitting an odd hum. At a loud signal that sounded like a berserk foghorn, the school children were taught to duck and cover, diving under their wooden desks and covering their small heads with their arms, as if fending off the attack of a nuisance dog. It was a festive exercise, disrupting spelling bees and multiplication tables.

Improvement was taking place everywhere: for the first time in memory, the city and county embarked on road projects. The men in the family discussed driving routes based on road maintenance detours. When the Caterpillars and pile drivers were raising a racket on Keaniani Street, Father went out to talk to the crew. Then he visited the neighbors. By the next day, he had collected enough cash to pay the road crew to roll down Keaniani Lane. At the end of a work day, around mid-afternoon, the crew rumbled along the lane, laying out a thick gravel bed and pressing it into place. Then they laid hot asphalt, followed by the rumbling steam roller. Everyone watched the dusty dirt lane transform into a neatly groomed cul-de-sac. One of the big machine drivers, an old-timer wearing a woman's straw hat and Hollywood sunglasses, even finessed a T-shaped turnaround at the end of the lane. The neighbor men threw in more cash and brought beer out for the crew. The women carried pans of fried rice and sweet and sour ribs. More trays and pans of goodies were passed around. The neighbor men and road crew mingled, laughing in the dusky light. The boys took chunks of blacktop and put them in their pockets. By dark, the lane was quiet, steam rising with the warm, sick smell of asphalt.

Everybody in town heard about the new Keaniani Lane (the mayor took credit for it and everybody laughed—he strolled around town in white pants and white shoes, shaking hands, remembering names). The dairyman in his squat blue and white step van stopped complaining about having to go around to the back of the house (to the door that was not nailed shut) to pick up and deliver milk bottles. He wanted details on the arrangement with the road crew; the neighbors on the lane referred him to the mayor's office. The slop man who came by once a week did not say anything but he nodded to Mother. She was one of the few people in town who collected clean slop for his pigs; the slop can hung on a pipe he had driven into the ground away from the house. When the honey wagon came by on its once-a-year mission to lower its hoses into the backyard cesspool, the two-man crew complimented Mother on the blacktop; they said it was better for their truck and equipment. Even the Fuller Brush man lingered, accepting a glass of beer and a beef and mayonnaise sandwich. Mother and Grandmother watched him eat; taking his time, he said more that afternoon than the men in their house said all week. After his wife and daughters left him, he took to sales work. He said that he had had his disappointments but somehow, no matter what, he still loved people. "People are people," he said. More salesmen found their way down the lane. Mother enjoyed answering the door, asking them to step inside.

Every Friday in the summer, the ice cream truck tinkled its tune and turned into the lane. Everyone knew the words to the tune:

Fortune's always hiding
I've looked everywhere

Fatso said that song was the story of his life. His pockets were full of coins, sagging with the weight of quarters, nickels, and dimes.

I'm forever blowing bubbles
Pretty bubbles in the air

Children stood next to the truck, studying the faded picture menu of various kinds of ice cream on a stick or neatly wrapped in paper. The driver leaned back in his busted seat, waiting, only the lurching idle of the engine suggesting that there were other places to go, other children standing around, dreaming of ice cream, inhaling the fumes of a small, hardworking truck. Fatso gave all the kids money to get their favorite, a nutty Drumstick, a Neapolitan sandwich, an orange Creamsicle.

Once a month, the mosquito truck pulled into the lane. It was a square black vehicle that puffed out clouds of DDT. Although mosquitoes were more a nuisance than a threat, their buzzing attacks could drive some people crazy. All the neighbors agreed that the smooth, black lane attracted a lot of attention. Thanks to the DDT program (and the uniformed boys who died of dengue fever), there were, in fact, many fewer mosquitoes, and families could relax in their patios on warm nights.

The children made fun of the truck driver. He drove slowly and waved at them, baring his blackened gums in a toothless grin. The truck did not look official. It had no city and county emblem and rattled like a jalopy, wheezing its way up and down the lane. The driver dangled his left arm out the door as if trolling water—a blind search for something, a slippery fish or fish-shadow with stunted, vestigial wings—his right arm barely steering, the truck making squeeze box noises, not a tune but random notes like birds on a wire.

Two boys in aloha shirt and t-shirt.

Coconut Grove flooded.

Another Warning

Sirens had been blaring for so long that no one heard them any more. Radio broadcasts repeated instructions to go to high ground and stay there. Streets winding uphill and homes with a view high above the bay were designated as safe. People in the flat Coconut Grove neighborhood left their homes and moved in a dense, antlike phalanx up the hill. Their empty houses looked like paper cutouts, tilting against the sky. A tree spread its branches, sagging with bunches of sweet, sticky plumeria. The line of cars going uphill was slow and wiggly. A man leaning out of his car window, flicking cigarette ash, smiled at two teenaged girls who walked with their arms entwined. An old Ford truck carried four boys on its running board. Whenever the truck stalled, the youngest boy hopped off and back on, laughing. The boys waved to the pedestrians as if they were in a parade.

Remembering the attack on Pearl Harbor, most of the adults were grateful that this was only a tsunami warning. There were oldsters who complained that they fled their homes too quickly, their stiff limbs and foggy thoughts rushed by sirens at dawn. Most people were still in their comfy bed clothes—faded muumuus and holey T-shirts, the soft rags of sleep and privacy. Only Mrs. Pomodor rushed down the hill to change into a nice daytime outfit, a polka dot shirt, capris, and high-heeled sandals. She said that it made her more alert and ready for the day. "It's worth the risk," she said to a woman wearing a towel like a shawl. "After all, I met my husband in the war."

At first, people politely knocked on doors to use the toilets of the homes on the hill, offering apologies for their kids or old folks. As the day went on, these residences became de facto relief stations for everything. Mr. and Mrs. Casella, retired school teachers who lived on a curving corner lot, made two huge pots of chili. One pot contained the wife's recipe, sweet and mild, and the other pot held the husband's, hot and spicy. Mr. Casella put on an apron and ladled chili into a Dixie cup for anybody who came by. "Hot or sweet?" he asked. He had a supply of Dixie cups in his garage and was glad to get rid of them.

By the afternoon, everyone looked familiar, as if their parked cars were little houses and all the people had arrived for the same party. Children roamed from their parents, even the little ones, looking for free

Popsicles or following their older cousins. People were leaning on cars, lucky ones sat in the shade—as if in a great silence, except that it was really under the long blasts of sirens.

"It started in the Aleutians, a volcano," one man said.

"I been there," another man said. "Silver salmon. Mild, pale, good eating."

As dusk fell, cooling the streets, people got back into their cars. Sirens continued to go on and off. The all clear signal had not been given, but some of the evacuees were heading down the hill. The fun had worn off, people were tired. Father looked for his son. "Ezra?" After a few beers, he wasn't in a hurry to collect his family. There were too many of them. He wasn't sure how everyone had fit into the car. He had enjoyed spending the day in the company of other men, holding a bottle of beer, talking in the street. As night fell, yellow porch lights were flicked on. The night air felt thinner than the daytime, sharp on the skin. Without further beckoning, the father's family members appeared, gravitating toward Mother, sitting with Grandmother on a blanket. The two girls rubbed their legs, feeling chilly in matching shorts. Uncle Fatso gave the girls a quarter each for being good all day. Auntie Gloria asked, "Where's my handsome boy?" She expected Ezra to instantly show up whenever she said that. "Hey, handsome," she called out. A rude whistle flew back from a passing car. Soon, Rene drifted back. Only Ezra was missing.

It was a long night for the family, looking for Ezra, alternately cursing and sighing for him. Father crisscrossed the hill, peering into the dark until his eyes felt like dry, rough pebbles. Mother and Grandmother sat in the car, waiting.

A mile away, in a wild, weedy field where the ground tilted up toward the mountain, Ezra was walking. His bare feet were tough, their soles stained the color of shoe leather. The air felt like petals on his face, his skinny legs humming with movement. He was following the sounds of a faraway ukulele. Earlier in the day, under full sun, the crowded street scene had pressed and squeezed the boy away from its hot center. All day long, his smallness had slipped through the spaces made by wide hips and bare legs. He was a bright blue ball in a pachinko machine, shooting through the levers that sang *ka-ching, ka-ching,* rolling along the easy switchbacks toward home. Although he knew that home was down the hill, he traced another line, the winding way in the dark. The boy felt, for the first time, as if he were on a voyage, the kind that calls for kisses and tears at the dock because no one would know when he would return. The thought of his mother waving a hanky, smiling through her tears, made him calm. If he were a grown man he would feel content, but he was only seven years old. On this night, he felt free of childish distractions.

The melody was plain, a single line of notes plucked on a string, resounding on smooth wood. The music rose and fell with the wind, pulling him toward a tent on a vacant lot. The lot was a holding pen for sand, gravel, and earthmoving equipment, surrounded by a cyclone fence. A metal sign on the fence said "KAPU! Keep out!" The tent had sprung up as testimony that this one day stood apart, an extraordinary day like a net cast out to sea, still floating, seeking its own shape. It was a two-peaked, high tent, the kind that serves as a summer home on the beach. From the outside, its white fabric ballooned out and sucked in with the wind.

It was brightly lit inside. Two large women sat on an old sofa, absentmindedly patting the sleeping children on their laps. An old woman leaned over them, covering the children's legs with small tea towels. There were two brothers strumming on ukuleles. The brothers were so big, solid as refrigerators, that the instruments looked like toys, their fingers picking out tunes with long, manicured nails. Everywhere Ezra turned, someone smiled at him. He walked over to a large table and sat under it. The table felt like a roof over his head. He folded himself into a compact shape, a box inside a box, fitted together and snapped shut. Drowsy, he toppled over.

The music felt warm, carrying the boy to a miniature island with a palm tree and grass hut on the sand. On this miniature, he fell fast asleep, a sleeping dot of a boy. The sleeping boy lived another life that night, songs of heartache, homesickness, young love, lost love, new and surprising love. The brothers sang as if they were talking to a friend. Swaying slightly as they sang, their wavy hair gleamed under lights strung on a slack line. The older brother closed his eyes and broke off into a girl's voice, a soft falsetto that climbed higher and higher, losing words. His girl's voice sounded like the kind of yearning that comes and goes with the wind.

Each person in the tent heard a different song, a private sense of what that tugging was, that longing for lost things. The sleeping boy grew into a young man and fell in love with a beautiful girl. They sailed to another island and settled on a farm, wading ankle deep in cold stream water to gather tall watercresses and hollow-stalked swamp grasses. They worked side by side from dawn till afternoon. Then they rested on a big, soft bed. The dream had unfolded the boy's body into a long ti leaf, his spine unfurled and supple with complete rest. At dawn, Ezra awoke, turned back into a boy.

Down the hill, out to the beach, the morning lay flat and quiet. There was no wind, no tide. The water had completely receded. A clear mile of the bay's floor was exposed; it was a strange sight that no one could compare to anything in memory.

On the wet stretch of sand, fishes were flopping everywhere. Ruts and ledges of sand, colorful rubber slippers here and there, seaweed clumped like gelatinous trees or light green and matted like hair, piles of pocked gray-white rocks, smooth green glass, shells that looked like ordinary gravel, and bits of trash that looked like precious jewels.

Word spread and a few people ventured out to see for themselves. There were many who were tired of waiting. Earlier feelings of dread were overrun by boredom. Among the restless, there was no expectation that waiting any longer would make a difference. Every passing hour added credence to their suspicion that endless waiting was for fools. The sky was clear blue. Birds were silent, out of sight.

By noon, it looked like the day before, people everywhere. A wave of people rushed from the highest hill to the bottom of the sea. Adults behaved like children, pointing and laughing.

Everyone wanted to start a collection. The bay turned into a concourse of opportunity, crawling with treasure hunters. There were more fish and 'ono seaweed than anybody could possibly gather. Buckets and wheelbarrows were not big enough to hold the harvest. Separating collectibles from garbage was exhausting guesswork, an impossible predicament of what to keep, what to throw away. People were picking through the littered expanse, relentless in their efforts, driven by the unforeseen opportunity. A bow-legged woman said that someone found a wedding ring with a diamond as big as a tooth. Radio broadcasts continued to issue warnings.

On a hill overlooking the bay, Mr. and Mrs. Casella were sitting in their kitchen, listening to the radio. *Fly me to the moon and let me play among the stars.* Mrs. Casella was secretly in love with Ol' Blue Eyes. She poured a cup of coffee for her husband. She made more coffee for the people still camped on their lawn.

When the wave train came, it rolled forward at over two hundred miles per hour. From the shore, it looked more like a wall of gray water. There was no cry or open mouth of surprise. It was an assault of weight like a locomotive of hissing steam and solid metal. The train rolled and pitched, drowning everything in sight. Then it rolled further up the shore, driving and hissing, flooding streets and houses, pushing upward. Water piled up and fell, over and over, until the island sank in despair. It took this moment of total submission to allow a slow and final retreat of that great train. The wave left a sodden stretch of tundra, potholes where trees once stood, dark shapes of standing water.

Radio programs were interrupted with estimated body counts and eyewitness reports. "Everything looked very small, people like bugs, cars like toys," one man said. There was no music on the radio, no strumming mele to accompany daily work. Armed forces reserves were called to action. Coast Guard ships were on standby.

All day, the family feared the worst, that the boy was washed out to sea. When the all clear signal was given, father bowed his head. In slow motion, the family gathered around him. Wordlessly, they squeezed into the Morris Minor to return home.

Piled on top of one another, no one spoke or squirmed for more room as Father drove down the hill. The sides of the small car seemed to give way so that Gloria, Fatso, Grandmother, and the girls could squeeze in the back seat. Thinking of her first husband bragging about a white horse with wings, Grandmother turned into a blue shadow, taking up no space at all. The girls intertwined their legs as if in sleep, making themselves into one. On family trips, Ezra usually sat between his mother's legs in the front seat. The family believed that the boy should see as much of the world as possible, even on a ride around town. Instead of the boy, Mother held Lucy up front, pressing her to her breast as if she were a stuffed pillow. The baby kept perfectly still, her eyes wide open above her mother's shoulder, looking at the faces in the back, the rhythmic chugging of the engine failing to lull her to sleep.

Their house stood as before, a white square with a pink concrete driveway. Grandfather, who had refused to evacuate, waved from the front yard. He was looking at the avocado tree, slung low with fruit—hard, immature footballs. He was waiting for one to ripen before his eyes. Grandfather's favorite snack was a halved avocado, its natural bowl filled with sugar. He would eat loudly, smacking his tongue against false teeth.

That night, Father switched off the television and everyone knew it was time to go to bed. When the family was together in the living room, watching TV and listening to the radio reporting the same news every ten minutes, they were bound by the outside narration of disaster, news reports quoting civil alert officials who gave the impression they were going to work around the clock to check and recheck the situation. It all sounded vaguely predictive, like weather reports, pointing toward a day when this would be left behind, a final report rounding up the names of persons lost and property damaged. For this reason, the adult members of the family were reluctant to retire to their own beds, expecting the reports to continue around the clock.

Alone, each person grew dull and weary, forgetting and then remembering why this night was strange, an odd sensation that the small house with many people was empty, missing the presence of the boy, his golden promise so much larger than his childish frame.

When Shorty felt lonely, it was for Eunice, not the boy. Shorty had just fled his own disaster—he had finally proposed marriage to Eunice and, smiling to herself, she shook her head, no, not the right time. Shorty turned around and left her, still shaking her head. Against roadblocks, he had raced over the Pali toward the scene of the tsunami, already feeling left out of the family's dilemma, their house trapped in the lowlands of Kailua Bay. It became clear to him that Eunice would never consent to marriage because she lacked the imagination to see the two of them together. Her head dipped down, she smiled to herself because she could not begin to imagine what she could not see. The next day and the days to follow, Shorty told himself that he would keep his eyes open for another and his ears attuned to a different voice, a voice that wondered why he liked the things he did, the reason why he preferred his coffee at room temperature (temperamental teeth) (this would make her laugh). Already he could hear a voice belonging to someone he had yet to meet, teasing him about his sensitive teeth, rising in laughter.

Because the boy was his, Father found no consolation in waiting, the business of waiting failing to spin thoughts in his head. When his wife was pregnant after the twins, round as a melon, he spent all of his waking hours wishing for a boy, silently and secretly because each girl was an awkward reminder of his constant wish that seemed to feed on itself, an embarrassing obsession for a man who can only plant the seed, the butt of family jokes about the seed that spelled g-i-r-l because his wife spelled b-o-s-s.

For all the waiting, Ezra's birth was just like the girls'. He wailed like a baby, louder and longer than Liz and Lana, flailing miserably until someone picked him up. The boy's special treatment was taken for granted, fulfilling an expectation that existed long before he was born. Everyone in the family cooperated, recognizing the emblem of a boy as shining and beyond compare. As Ezra grew up, father wished to keep him close by, no, to push him away, to somehow prepare him for the world, keeping him to himself, sending out another boy in his place, a boy spirit flung out to sea. Ezra's obedience galled his father. Where was the famous Korean temper? The kind of hot temper that causes grown men to drink too much, gamble their paychecks, double their losses? Even as the boy followed him around, learning his tricks, he sensed that the kid had already packed up his bags and left home.

Rubbing his wife's pregnant belly for good luck, he did not know that all a father does in the life of a child is wait. While he's waiting, there's a lot to do—going to the office, paying the bills, fixing up the house—no matter how fast or slow time goes by, it all amounts to the same thing.

His wife lay in bed next to him, awake but wordless. Sitting up in bed, Father's mouth was dry, no spit rose up in his throat, as if he would be without anything to say for the rest of his life. Looking into the dark room, seeing nothing in particular, he forgot about his ordeal.

Stuck with sentry duty in the middle of nowhere, he remembered scrambling to his post, pulling up his pants, running with his boot laces dragging in the muck. Breathless, he signaled the other sentry to retire for the night. The other soldier was a kid like himself, watching his desperate attempts to pull himself together with buckles and laces, breaking out in helpless glee. They gasped with muffled delight, holding onto each other's shoulders so neither would fall down. Breaking the silence of sentry duty could have gotten them both killed.

Father looked at his wife who was looking at him. This time he would not lapse into fatigued hijinks. He lifted the white sheet and got out of bed. Standing in his bare feet, looking out the window, he would try not to get the boy killed.

Up the hill in the tent, Ezra sat under the table, watching the old woman make coffee. The dented metal pot rocked with a head of steam, perked coffee spurting into the hollow glass knob on top. The other children noticed the boy for the first time and joined him under the table. A girl with a round face, small and flat as a coin, stared at the boy. She looked at him for a long while, until she felt satisfied. The grownup brother with the girl's voice called out, "Eh-ay, you the one." The big man gave him a sweet bun. The boy asked for another bun, wishing to stay, having grown attached to the two singing brothers. They hummed a few more songs as they finished packing up the tent. Others loaded furniture and boxes of goodies onto their trucks and cars, waving goodbye.

"Blallah, take care, now."

"Eh, you too."

The vehicles U-turned slowly in the lot, stirring up brown puffs of dirt.

"Where you live?" the soft-voiced brother asked. He handed Ezra a bottle of orange soda to drink in the car. The other brother was so relaxed, he could steer the car with his belly. It was a trick that made the boy laugh. Riding home, he sucked on the nubby glass lip of the bottle, pointing out the way.

The girls shrieked uncontrollably when they spotted their brother standing in the driveway, waving to a departing car. There were no harsh words for Ezra, just tears rolling down everyone's cheeks. Although he was a gangly child and really too big to be lifted off his feet, he was carried all day long. Uncle Fatso carried him on his hip and kissed his sweaty head. Father carried him on his back, as if he were a sack of rice. The girls made a sedan chair with their locked arms, carrying him around the living room. All day, somebody carried him. It wasn't until nightfall when everyone sat down to dinner that he was released. At the table, taking his place next to Father, his feet finally touched the ground.

The third day began with purpose after the endless waiting and chaos of the tsunami. It started with a few boys who surveyed the mess; they huddled and emerged with a plan. The boys worked steadily, sorting through the debris, drawing lines in the sand with sticks. After that, various groups formed to collect different things. The impetus to make tidy piles and rows of things spread among the children. Day after day, they picked up and carried things, making hills of seashells and building mountains of beach toys— plastic tubes shrunk and crinkled, deflated balls, buckets, shovels, dolls—and more than anything else, shoes of all kinds.

Clouds of black flies latched onto mounds of garbage. The flies ate and respired in unison, droning with pleasure. A bare-chested man with flowing hair made a bonfire of felled trees. He stood there all day, throwing rafts of palm fronds onto the low, smoldering flames. It was a mournful slag fire that spewed black smoke and clouds of ashes.

When school reopened, the children reluctantly left their work in unfinished patterns. The beach was roped off as a hazardous area. Signs were installed. Restoration took place as a paramilitary operation. Backhoes, Caterpillars, and trucks gobbled up the children's neat piles and rows. Between the shore and the hills, the tsunami's erasure was gradually filled in. The governor made a pledge that "the zone of destruction will be made over into a *Hawaiian style* Garden of Eden." Everything ended up as landfill, a multi-layered midden.

Over time, the landfill cooked and settled into real estate. It was paved and seeded with green grass. Grids of power and water were installed. A canal with sloping concrete sides ran a straight line from the houses to the sea. Realty ads said, "You can go fishing in your own back yard!" Baby palm trees were planted. The brand new houses were charming, painted pastel colors of the rainbow with white trim.

The developers named the tract *Lili'uokalani Park*. Kids called it *da zone.* "Eh, meet chu at da zone." Families pooled their savings and put as many relatives as possible under one roof. Everyone watered their lawns to a perfect, spiky emerald green. An odd smell sometimes emanated from the grass. The midden continued to cook beneath, forming methane fumes that seeped through the carpet of green. Authorities said it was safe, but children should not play with matches. People were encouraged to barbecue only on concrete slabs or in their driveways.

Whenever that odd smell arose, neighborhood boys would slip away in groups of twos and threes. Each boy carried a book of matches in his pocket. They would crawl on their hands and knees, sniffing the ground, then lower themselves flat, dragging their length like combat soldiers. Lighting up, a boy would roll over, face down, then jump up and run. One after another, in an invisible cloud of methane, they would ignite flash fires. "Kill the Japs! Get 'em, get 'em!" Strike a match: *Flash!* A smoking brown spot on the ground smelled like a burning body. *Flash! Flash!* Leaping with joy, the boys would run at top speed; they ran in packs around fields and parking lots; eventually, with stomachs growling for hot rice, they ran in smaller and smaller circles that zeroed in on their homes. After running so hard, the boys ate savagely. Their mothers refilled their plates and praised them for their grunting appetite.

Two boys, accountable to nobody, were spending the night on Flat Island, a patch of rock ledges and scrubby growth in the middle of the bay. Their flimsy pup tent was propped up against the wind, rattling against a scrawny bush. They had walked out to the island during low tide, carrying boxes of camping gear on their heads. The older boy convinced the younger that they were *defending* the island from invasion. They ate canned meat for dinner and washed it down with beer. From this tiny island, the shore dotted with houses seemed far away. Lanikai Point loomed in their sights, a lava cliff that reached its fingers into thin air.

The black promontory absorbed the shock of white, foaming waves. Fishes slowly circled and slept in the bay. With the trees bending toward the water and the water lapping onto the shore, what was suggested is the way one receives the other. Across the beach road, people withdrew into their houses that were lit like lanterns against the night. Recent rains had raised the level of the canal connecting to the bay. The canal water was thick and brown, emptying at a wide mouth into the bay waters.

Near the mingling of waters, only one fish jumped and flopped. An old and ugly tilapia from the canal was breaking surface, gulping air. A tough, scar-faced bottom feeder, the fish was no prize. It jumped again, a stubborn effort, an impulse. Near the mouth of the canal where the brown waters fanned out and slid into the bay, it jumped and flopped for the last time. Landing on wet sand, it lay panting.

A light rain fell, sprinkling the old thing until its mottled skin glistened. Enough water fell from the sky to make it gasp for more, but not enough to carry it out to sea.

Kailua Bay.

Love a Stranger

Like common sand crabs, public projects moved forward, backward, sideways. People forgot the rationale for a borrowed fortune spent on roads and buildings, the tsunami becoming yet another story. Some of the plans for restoration were scrapped because of the natural order of things: the quick succession from mud to grass to thick creepers with fig-shaped leaves took place without municipal planting. Cars clogged with sand, so many stuck along roads, were indistinguishable from the ones parked for the time being, according to convenience. An Edsel filled with rich sea silt grew creepers through its front grille. Children climbed in through the open front door windows, pretending to drive to Honolulu. Filled with sand or not, most of the cars looked ready to go somewhere.

It seemed as if only moments had passed before Ezra had grown into a young man, leaving the islands under the weight of fragrant flower lei. Standing on the tarmac before ascending the metal staircase to the plane, he already looked like a stranger to his family. The faces he had watched so closely, each one as round as a coin, imprinted with lines and soft hair, now looked like a single visage, a bulging crowd of tearful well wishers.

The twins had grown tall and slender on an all-American diet of bologna sandwiches and milk. They held handkerchiefs, facing each other with wet eyes, drawn together in a trance that would carry them to the next daydream, always a fixed object of desire designed for both, each taking the other's fixity as her own.

Everyone stayed to watch Ezra climb up and disappear into the plane then reappear at a porthole window, waving.

Taught that he was different from all others, Ezra concluded that he could not stay with his family, following in his father's footsteps, taking over the house in due time. Instead, he would go to California and live with strangers, eventually losing his palate for hot spicy foods, preferring to eat in restaurants, making eyes at healthy girls with good teeth and an outgoing sense of humor. For Father, losing his son to California was worse than losing him to war. Father regretted the fact that he treated his son as a golden child, separating him from other children with special duties and rewards. It felt like robbery to be left with a houseful of girls and two middle-aged men who behaved like women, blaming their situation on bad luck and lousy timing.

The golden child is forever golden only in the eyes of his maker; to everyone else, he is a traitor, plying a pair of finely wrought, antique scissors to cut the thread of life, that slippery line from the mother all bloody and black, joining and holding, a cursive knot unfurled. Once severed, the black line leaks the juices of life, in a matter of days, curling into a tough runty stem.

Although this may seem like a harsh way to remember a beloved family member, it is also as natural as the changing tides. Like everyone else in the islands, the family knows how repetitive and relentless the lapping of the waves is, wearing down the sharp edges of certainty. There are days of forgetfulness when the shore is not a friend of the sea, and the tall royal palms do not bend toward the battered shore, and the waters roil and plunge without reference to a white placid moon in a pale blue sky. Those are the days of forgetfulness, the days of wandering in hunger and thirst, not wishing for anything more than a little something to eat, drink, and upon imagining those things, wishing further, for nothing in particular. A bird flaps across an ocean to reach land, a green stick for a perch, that is all.

Gloria wavered between dreams, days of continuous embarrassments and adjustments, years without the privacy of a closed door, her legs sticking out beyond the colorful scarf, her ankles and small feet bare and wriggling in sleep. Gloria lost her love for family. Her love did not turn into something else; rather, it grew large and moved out of the house. In a town where everyone knew who she was, she walked around looking for a stranger. She missed Dante. For him, she had a reason to wash her hair. He gave her something he did not know that he possessed, something that radiated from his fierce, solemn look, perhaps the remnant of his love for his mother (whatever it was, it could be punted over the hedge all the way to her high window). Her love for him was as fixed as a nail in a board.

She missed him but found company with strangers, mostly the customers in the store who asked questions and seemed curious about everything around town. Instead of walking home, she took to wandering along the beach, taking off her fancy slippers, digging her feet into the sand. She could see the curving shape of the bay, the wet, shallow shelf of life, and the deeper blue of its dropping off, the suggestion that somewhere the horizon disappears, voiding distinctions between sea and sky.

A sea turtle swam in shallow water, young, with faint shell markings, playing in the waves. Gloria looked as it paddled and splashed. She looked until she realized that the turtle had been swept away, out of sight. She felt no need to wander any further. Soon enough it would be time to sit at the dinner table with her brothers, sister, her sister's husband, the girls, her old mother.

Maybe Toots and Lovey will drop by. Someone said they were coming back after all these years. That Lovey had a bad back, lost his job. Rene would show up and fall into his own silhouette, softly shaped on stained, flattened cushions. The old sofa looked for the lost boy.

There were places inside the house, not the center of things but around them, that looked for its inhabitants. A procession of dime-store ceramic figures crowded the kitchen window sill, a pig, sheep, horses, a girl with a bonnet, waiting for Mother to rearrange them in an order that followed a road to a big old barn. After washing the dinner dishes, Mother sometimes could not stop wiping things down, folding and patting the dish towels, moving the painted figures of animals around, pointing them the other way. No matter which way they were facing, the sheep kept their noses close to the ground. The two coffee tables in the living room held so many things that the objects could only look up, sideways would have caused a riot of disorder—a Kleenex box next to a heavy glass ashtray, dishes of candy, an empty cookie canister, what was offered and what was already taken, side by side, cluttering the two tables.

Like trees above a valley, the things in a room transpire. Surfaces of things we see and touch every day grow blank faces when we are not around, shedding the sticky warmth of our fingers, the sentimental attachment of our eyes. If we go, these things remain, like the permanence of large-scale things outside, the steep green hills and the sandy curve of the bay. These things are the befallen, the given. When we return, the lucky ones who don't drop off into the sea, we look and take what we want. Stacked up the slopes, forming a densely green V above the busy valley floor, the trees are pushing water and air outward, into the mist, forcing vapor into the blue. Empty rooms rest so they can receive us at the end of the day.

Gloria was hoping that no one was watching television at home; she wouldn't mind having the living room to herself. A short nap in its cool dim light would be nice.

If there were a lull at the dinner table, she had a good story to tell, about the customer who asked for brown bread in a can. He had a drooping moustache and wore soft cotton clothes the color of brown bread, looking sad and kind, smelling of pipe tobacco. He said he misses a meal of brown bread, pushed out of a can, spread with warm baked beans. He said this was especially good after a day sailing around the bay. Sailing around, of course, in a boat! The thought of a wooden boat with a white sail sounded lonely, forever dipping in the waves, rocking its occupant gently, until it is dragged onshore. The man had trailed his sadness from another shore, cold ocean water on one side and warm pond water on the other, beds with tucked sheets, extra blankets piled high. Beans on bread, of course, could be consolation for a very tired sailor. She wondered why he seemed so tired, eating food that looked like small wooden logs.

Bread in a can! Gloria laughed at the thought and hurried home.

Reader's Guide

Note to Teachers and Book Groups

The background information and questions that follow are designed to spark discussion in the classroom or with your book group. Since the novella offers life sketches in a historical context, you're invited to offer your own stories—memories of a formative decade, family life against a historical and cultural backdrop.

Of Time and Place

This story takes place in Kailua on the island of O'ahu, a small town built around a crescent-shaped bay marked by a black lava promontory called Lanikai Point. It's the early 1950s in the Territory of Hawai'i (before statehood), after World War II and during the Korean War.

Historical and Cultural Context

Although historical figures such as General MacArthur and Norman Vincent Peale *(The Power of Positive*

Thinking) occasionally appear, the heart of the story lies with a large, multigenerational Korean-American family living under one roof—immigrant grandmother and grandfather, mother, father, children Lana, Liz, Ezra, Lucy, cousin Rene, auntie Gloria, uncles Fatso and Shorty.

The tenor of the story is one of war fatigue bearing down on a desire to think positively, to walk on the sunny side of the street, to be a good American. In WWII, Hawai'i residents enlisted in record numbers, including the all-Japanese 442nd combat regiment ("Go for broke") sent to the European front, known as the most decorated unit in U.S. military history. Hawai'i's soldiers in the Korean War fought against an enemy who physically resembled themselves—Chinese, Japanese, Koreans—but in U.S. uniforms. (Later, during the Vietnam War, Hawai'i soldiers would continue to contribute their outsize share to overseas deployment, no longer in "segregated" units like the 442nd.)

The story is a miniature—house, island, world. In spite of public messages of optimism, this Korean-American family is sagging under the weight of daily necessity, missing the coattails of the American Dream. It's a small house and a small world, full of the particulars of immigrant family life—hot and spicy Korean food, how neighbors grudgingly get along, how a boy mentally packs his bags long before leaving home.

Discussion Questions

1) "...Arthur Godfrey is coming to town! With his hit songs and ukulele!" (Prologue, 2). If Hawai'i is the

home of the ukulele, why would local people so admire a haole mainland celebrity who popularized the happy sounds of the "uke"? If Godfrey's radio and television shows were a mirror, what did Hawai'i people hear and see in this?

How did post-war media, especially syndicated television *(Ozzie and Harriet)* and *Playboy* magazine, change American culture—and how did island people see themselves, *apart* from or *part of* these images?

2) "...fine cotton pillow cases edged with crocheted points...a crystal punch bowl with twelve cups and a curved ladle" (Inside a Cedar Chest, 27). Gloria's hope chest was a social convention of unmarried women who accumulated household treasures for their future marriage. In what ways did these things symbolize what Gloria was hoping for?

Another convention was referring to an older, unmarried woman as an Old Maid. There was even a popular card game by that name, the loser being the one stuck with the Old Maid card. How have the traditions of marriage and family changed? Stayed the same?

3) "Unlike Gloria, Shorty did not believe in the power of positive thinking." (From the Hedge to the Street, 53). Why were Norman Vincent Peale's radio and television shows on positive thinking so popular? During and after the war, why was optimism often associated with patriotism?

In terms of promise and delivery, what were the consequences—public and private—of selling the American brand of optimism in political speeches and TV evangelism?

4) "Like other local boys, they preferred the privileges of the uniform in place of their white T-shirts..." (Black Hair, White Wings, 75). What were the presumed privileges of wearing a military uniform? Without the uniform, what penalties could a local guy expect?

Immediately after the Japanese attack on Pearl Harbor, the Territory of Hawai'i was placed under martial law since Japanese residents were classified as enemy aliens and it wasn't feasible to turn all of the islands into one big internment camp. In spite of this, many local residents, including the Japanese, enlisted for combat duty. Why?

In today's volunteer armed services, who are targeted by recruitment campaigns as most likely to enlist? Who are the boots-on-the-ground serving in Iraq and Afghanistan?

5) "Even moments of anxiety seemed routinely scheduled: once a month, civil defense sirens blared for a full minute at noon" (Civil Alert, 112). During the Cold War years, school children were taught to "duck and cover" in case of nuclear attack. How do we cope with modern anxieties such as nuclear war? Terrorism?

In the wake of the Pearl Harbor attack—and again after 9/11—we sensed a shift of consciousness about our world. And given what we now know about climate change, irreversible damage to our blue-green island, Planet Earth, feels imminent. How have our ideas on attack and defense, danger and protection changed over time?

6) "That night Ezra sat at the table wearing his coonskin cap…drinking chocolate milk…" (From the Hedge to the Street, 53). Those Americans who lived through the Depression and WWII have been described as the Greatest Generation and successive generations as the Spoiled Generation or the Me Generation. Do you agree or disagree with these characterizations?

Well before our current sense of ethnic and cultural identities and the 1970s Hawaiian Renaissance, local people sacrificed so that their children could grow up all-American. In what ways did statehood usher in the notion that "now we're all haoles"?

Excepting Native Americans and Native Hawaiians, everyone's an immigrant in this country—what's your family story?

7) "Everybody in town heard about the new Keaniani Lane (the mayor took credit for it and everybody laughed…" (Civil Alert, 114). How does local humor instantly deflate power and authority? How do local people "go around" rules and regulations in order to "make do" from day to day?

And how does this relate to Native American "serious joke medicine" and African-American "dozens" and country music lyrics ("I forgot to remember to forget her") to get us through the day? How does humor relieve us of bad news or human error?

8) "Taught that he was different from all others," Ezra concluded that he could not stay with his family..." (Love a Stranger, 140). "...Gloria lost her love for family..." (141). For different reasons, both Ezra and Gloria grow away from the family. Ezra leaves. Gloria stays. Why? And why does Gloria have an insatiable fascination with strangers? What quality leads her to strangers from far away?

In widening circles—from family to community to country to the world—is it possible to love a stranger as a family member or a friend? In the case of war, famine, natural disaster, are we responsible for strangers living far away from us? Can we take more swimmers into our lifeboat? Or, do we turn away?

Suggested Reading

Appiah, Kwame Anthony. *Cosmopolitanism: Ethics in a World of Strangers.* New York: W. W. Norton, 2006.
Crisscrossing continents, Appiah combines his personal story of mixed heritage with a philosophical contemplation of our sense of identity, authenticity, and greater humanity.

Chang, Roberta (with Wayne Patterson). *The Koreans in Hawaii: A Pictorial History 1903-2003.* Honolulu: University of Hawai'i Press, 2003.
Photos tell the story of each decade's wave of new immigrants and, notably, Hawai'i-born Koreans in the Korean War.

Daws, Gavan. *Shoal of Time.* Honolulu: University of Hawai'i Press, 1974 (PB).
A vivid, single-volume history of Hawai'i from Captain Cook's arrival to statehood.

Daws, Gavan and Bennett Hymer, ed. *Honolulu Stories.* Honolulu: Mutual Publishing, 2008.
An anthology of many voices spanning 200 years, a mix of renowned visitors (Mark Twain, Robert Louis Stevenson, Herman Melville) and ethnically diverse

Hawai'i writers (Nora Okja Keller, Cathy Song, Kiana Davenport, Lois Ann Yamanaka, Chris McKinney).

Foster, Jenny Ryun, Frank Stewart, and Heinz Insu Fenkl. *Century of the Tiger: One Hundred Years of Korean Culture in America, 1903-2003*. Honolulu: Manoa Journal, Centennial Committee of Korean Immigration to the United States, University of Hawai'i Press, 2003.
A large-format photo and art album with commentary, stories, poems that chart the arrival and continuing negotiation of Korean culture in America.

Kailua Historical Society, ed. *Kailua: Ke Oho O Ka Malanai, In the Wisps of the Malanai Breeze*. Kailua: Kailua Historical Society, 2009.
Beautifully designed by Barbara Pope, a large-format volume of photographs, maps, commentary focused on the Hawaiian concept of ahupua'a, a pie-shaped land use pattern that runs from a high watershed of mountain to flat, sandy beaches—an ancient, self-sustaining way to live on the land.

Okihiro, Gary Y. *Island World: A History of Hawaii and the United States*. Berkeley: University of California Press, 2008.
This book challenges the assumed polarities of island and continent, vast ocean and landmass, migration and settlement—tracing the influence of a far-flung Hawaiian diaspora.

Patterson, Wayne. *The Ilse: First-Generation Korean Immigrants in Hawaii, 1903-1973*. Honolulu:

University of Hawai'i Press, 2001.
Primary sources—Japanese surveillance records, student journals, and U.S. intelligence reports— provide a little-known narrative of Korean experiences as plantation laborers, Christian mission workers, picture brides, city merchants.

Robbins, Trina, ed. *Forbidden City: the Golden Age of Chinese Nightclubs.* Cresskill, NJ: Hampton Press, 2010.
Photographs and interviews with entertainers from the 1930s to the 1950s—how Asian men and women fashioned themselves after American stars like Ginger Rogers and Fred Astaire, and notably, Frank Sinatra, Ol' Blue Eyes.

More Resources

Links

Popular music from the Territory era on vinyl 78s, 45s, 33 1/3 LPs
http://hawaiian105.com/markets/honolulu/ ads/09territorial-airwaves.html

Online vintage radio with Lucky Luck and others
http://hawaiian105.com/MARKET/shared/ads/ territorial_airwaves.html

Vintage photos of Hawai'i landmarks and informal commentary
http://www.kalihikids.com/OldHawaii/

Ordinary people write about growing up in Hawai'i
http://www.hawaiireporter.com/list.aspx?Growing+Up +in+Hawaii+Series

Aloha Airlines film promotion about Hawai'i, 1950
http://www.youtube.com/watch?v=dSAGFcteW3E

Hearst newsreel on Hawai'i in the 1950s, introducing the 50th state
http://www.youtube.com/watch?v=kP1GchaSO1A&fea ture=channel

Honolulu Chinatown film clip from the 1950s
*http://www.youtube.com/watch?v=cBZJuKLpvF4&fea
ture=related*

Movies

Zinnemann, Fred, dir. *From Here to Eternity.* Columbia
Pictures, dist., 1953.
Adaptation of James Jones' novel about military
life in the islands before the attack on Pearl Harbor
and the onset of war. With Burt Lancaster, Deborah
Kerr, Montgomery Clift, Frank Sinatra, Donna Reed,
Ernest Borgnine.

Perier, Etienne, dir. *A Bridge to the Sun.* Metro-
Goldwyn-Mayer, dist., 1961.
Adaptation of Gwen Terasaki's 1957 novel about
the love and marriage of an Asian man and Western
woman, a Hollywood breakthrough, with Hawai'i-
born James Shigeta and Carroll Baker.

Adachi, Jeff, dir. *The Slanted Screen.* AAMM
Productions, 2006.
Documentary on WTAG or "Where's the Asian
Guy?"—the absence or subordination of the Asian
male in the media, especially the movies.

Hit songs, 1950-1953

Mona Lisa, Nat King Cole, 1950
Tennessee Waltz, Patti Page, 1950

My Foolish Heart, Billy Eckstine, 1950
Dear Hearts and Gentle People, Bing Crosby, 1950
Come On-a My House, Rosemary Clooney, 1951
How High the Moon, Les Paul & Mary Ford, 1951
It's No Secret, Inkspots, 1951
Jezebel, Frankie Laine, 1951
Cry, Johnnie Ray, 1952
A Guy Is a Guy, Doris Day, 1952
Walkin' My Baby Back Home, Johnnie Ray, 1952
With These Hands, Eddie Fisher, 1953
Don't Let the Stars Get in Your Eyes, Perry Como,
     1953
C'est Si Bon, Eartha Kitt, 1953
Shake, Rattle and Roll, Bill Haley & the Comets
     (1954)—rock'n'roll arrives

1950s Pop Culture

Nylon stockings and lipstick—Revlon's Fire & Ice,
Cherries in the Snow, Fifth Avenue Red

Cars and highways—Cadillac and Corvette, Disneyland,
McDonald's, Howard Johnson

Television—Edward R. Murrow's *See It Now, Roy
Rogers, Flash Gordon, Dragnet*

Playboy magazine—girl-next-door nudity, the celebrity
interview, social libertarianism

Television evangelism, biblical epic movies—church membership skyrockets

Rock'n'roll—"teenager" enters the lexicon

Baby boom—Benjamin Spock, a baby born every 7 seconds

Suburbs—conventions of work and family, well-defined gender roles

American Dream—consumerism, TV advertising

Cereal box prizes—Captain Midnight secret-decoder ring, rubber-band balsa-wood airplane

Corporation—*The Man in the Gray Flannel Suit* (book and movie), automation of work

Science—IBM mainframe, hydrogen bomb, Salk vaccine

Fantasy—UFO sightings, Hollywood space alien movies, Ray Bradbury's *Martian Chronicles*

Timeline

Territory of Hawaiʻi to Statehood

1893
U.S. overthrow of Queen Liliʻuokalani.

1898
Annexation of the former Kingdom of Hawaiʻi as part of the U. S. doctrine of Manifest Destiny.

1900
Territory of Hawaiʻi government established by the Hawaiian Organic Act.

1900s
Sugarcane plantations and the Big Five corporations control the economy and government—Castle & Cooke, Alexander & Baldwin, C. Brewer, Amfac, Theo H. Davies.

1901
Dole pineapple plantation and cannery established.

1908
Matson begins passenger service on the steamer *Lurline* between San Francisco and Honolulu.

1908-1909
Ft. Shafter, Pearl Harbor, Schofield military bases installed. Military assumes position of power and influence alongside the Big Five.

1927
Royal Hawaiian Hotel, "the pink palace," opens for business.

Dedicaton St. Luke's Church.

Hundred-day-old baby celebration at St. Luke's.

1931
Massie trial—five Hawaiians falsely accused of raping the wife of a naval officer.

1941
Japan's attack on Pearl Harbor.

1941-1944
Territory of Hawai'i placed under martial law with a military governor installed to replace a dissolved civilian government.

1950-1953
Korean War.

Pineapple workers.   Kailua town.

1952
Hawaiʻi KGMB television station launched.

Local TV goes live with the *Lucky Luck Show*—"Lucky you come Hawaiʻi."

Arthur Godfrey on syndicated radio and TV, sponsored by Lipton Tea and Frigidaire.

Norman Vincent Peale's *The Power of Positive Thinking* is a bestseller, followed by shows on radio and television.

Kailua Shopping Center.   Papaya grove.

1954

Widespread worker strikes and shift of power from Republicans to Democrats in the islands.

Sunrise with Kini Popo and Peaches the chimp, local talk show often featuring celebrities on vacation—"Right on the Kini Popo."

1959

Hawai'i becomes the 50th state, the admission act signed by President Dwight Eisenhower.

TV comes to Hawai'i.

Radio personality Kini Popo a.k.a. Carl Hebenstreit.

Interview with
the Author

Q. What initially made you want to tell this story?
A. I wasn't sure at first...Auntie Gloria came to mind early on, but the story unfolded as I started to write. Once the first draft was done, it emerged as a tribute to my parents' generation, those who lived through the Depression and World War II...doing whatever they could to make a better life for their children. Next to my parents, my own life feels far less vivid, too soft, too accommodating of injustice.

Q. Why do you think it's important to tell this story?
A. The passing of generations and of times gone by often feel like a vague seasickness, an indescribable sense of loss—we want to get our bearings but don't know how. Even though we know there's no such thing as turning back the clock, we can trick time by telling stories. For the duration of the telling, we can fulfill our wish to live those days again. So much of story telling is about wishing it all back again.

Q. Any reason you chose Kailua as the locale?

A. Since I grew up in Kailua, there's a memory map that I can draw from. After all these years, Kailua has kept its small town character, resisting high-rises. Kailua's crescent-shaped bay and its roads radiating from an old banyan tree feel like a garden, something to behold and take care of. If we can remember it, we'll protect this place.

Q. Why the 1950s? To young people, that's ancient history! What are the benefits of having your story take place in another era?

A. To begin with, I grew up in the fifties...and the tug of memory can be more deeply felt as an adult remembering what it was like as a child. Curiously, kids today seem drawn to '50s kitsch and tchotchkes, stuff of seemingly simpler times. And we tend to think of news, what's happening now, to be factual and documented...but recollections from memory allow the dynamic of fact and fiction to create a disturbance, telling lies to get closer to the truth, inventing larger landscapes and crises of the heart.

Q. How did you draw from real life to create your characters?

A. That's a tricky question—as I was writing, the characters multiplied and crowded my mind—on the page, more and more people pushed their way into this small house, like an overstuffed suitcase. This created a new character for me, the family— an ensemble of characters instead of one central figure. By avoiding a typical situation, I could dare to create characters that were both true to life and richly fictive—to make the ordinary something extraordinary.

Q. Do you foresee a sequel taking the family into a later time period?

A. No, there's no intent for that. The fifties seemed a bit slower and sweeter than the sixties and onward, but just below the surface simmered huge changes. What a story can do is deliver the *then* and *now* altogether, collapsing and tricking time. This story feels slow cooked and done.

Q. How was the Korean immigration story any different from the Chinese or Japanese?

A. Growing up, I remember checking the box "other" for ethnicity; there didn't seem to be as much of an aggregate of Koreans. Our paternal grandparents, who were immigrants, lived with us and preferred speaking English, especially our grandmother, who wanted to learn slang from us grandchildren. Our dad used to say that the Koreans were the Irish of the East, hard-drinking and hot-tempered, and that Korea was like Poland, constantly getting run over and occupied by outsiders. All this a set-up for why Koreans are so sly and stubborn—always in survival mode. When our mom called our dad "yobo" (slang for Korean) this could be a cooing love call or, at other times, an epithet, suggesting a rogue or bum. We kids heard it as a tough love nickname.

Q. How do famous people like General Douglas MacArthur and Norman Vincent Peale serve the story?

A. Yes, that's exactly what they do, they *serve* the story. What I love about fiction is its freedom—in this case, pushing historical figures to the background and bringing forward ordinary people, making it *our* story, *our* thoughts, *our* dreams that prevail.

Q. *If You Live in a Small House* is designated as a novella by your publisher. How is a novella different from a novel? And why did your book turn out this way?

A. To begin with, we can think of this as a short novel with a long title! Novellas traditionally run somewhere between 20,000 to 50,000 words—Faulkner's *The Bear*, Hemingway's *The Old Man and the Sea,* Dickens' *A Christmas Carol*...the Russians loved the form, Dostoevsky, Tolstoy, Chekhov...and more recently, *Breakfast at Tiffany's* by Truman Capote, *The House on Mango Street* by Sandra Cisneros, *Push* by Sapphire.

Novellas are often compared to movies and stage plays because they can be experienced in one sitting. *Small House* is a work of memory, and memory can pick and choose, offering appetizer and dessert, skipping meat and potatoes—rushing to a fullness of feeling. Even in its spare state, I didn't hesitate to cut, cut, cut anything that detracted from the core, the heart of the matter.

Q. When did you start writing?

A. Soon after I learned to read—birthday cards for family members, school work, and at around age 10, letters to pen pals around the world. Letter writing was a form of diary and autobiography—a naïve form of narrative within reach of my child's view of the world...teen angst fed the flames of bad sonnets and moody stories...in college I tried playwriting just because I spent so much time in the theatre department, mostly working backstage. My writing life developed parallel to a work life, keeping a day job, writing on the side. In middle age, I exited Silicon Valley and went back to school. That's when I finally felt permission to read and write to my heart's content.

Q. That's a long time to wait, to get to do what you wanted all along. Do you feel as if real life conspired to keep you from writing?

A. Surprisingly, this turned out to be a good thing. Necessity dictates improvisation. Each job led to a different world—as a technical writer, to fieldwork on the North Slope of Alaska and to national parks in California, Nevada, Arizona, Hawai'i. In London, I worked as a telephonist, in the days when long-distance calls had to be patched into a switchboard, talking with callers and relay operators. When a student, I worked as a pineapple trimmer at Dole cannery and as a cocktail waitress at the Green Turtle and the Blue Dolphin Room in Waikiki. Working puts you into the stream of life, providing raw material for stories.

Q. What about your other real-life milestones?

A. Well, I was born and raised in Hawai'i—grew up in Kailua, attended the University of Hawai'i, left to travel and work abroad, met my husband in San

Francisco. Since 1971, we've lived in the San Francisco Bay Area, raising three children who are now all grown up. When they were young, my kids were the recycle police; now they're teaching me so much more, that moral outrage is not just for the young and the restless.

Q. Which writers influenced your work? Who are your favorites?

A. As a child, fairy tales cast a spell, a way to experience heightened, oftentimes gruesome, emotions—even now, it's hard to predict whether toads or pearls will fall from my character's lips! Reading Sherwood Anderson and Eudora Welty for the first time, I remember thinking, "Ah, just like small town Hawai'i!" Anderson lived in boarding houses, closely observing how people constantly negotiated a limited space and loss of privacy. Welty never married, liked ice-cold Coke in heat and humidity, finely forming sentences that entered the ear and lodged in the heart. Oddly, I have no favorites. Far better to read widely and a lot, across time, across cultures. Right now, I'm reading more history and poetry, leaving fiction up to TV news—this world is stranger than fiction.

Q. What advice would you give an aspiring writer?

A. Welcome! You're already a writer. To begin with, we are our first readers—we write something, then read it before anyone else. Sei Shonagon wrote *The Pillow Book* as a bored, distracted young woman in the Heian Court of the early 1000s, private writing that time-travels to us as a classic, suggesting early novelistic touches. Reading sows the seeds of writing—we not only draw from real life but from the world of imagination. As John Ruskin put it, reading is seeing clearly. So what if there's no consolation for loss, as long as we can locate that loss and see with our inner eye, the one tied to our soul.

Q. That sounds so sad. Anything upbeat you could add to that?
A. Not really. You're talking to someone who fell in love with longing and homesickness…where the heart lives…writing in order to find one's home.

Photo Credits

Hawai'i's public archives and museums, augmented by private collectors, do an excellent job of maintaining photo collections. It is through their efforts and cooperation that the photos in this book were gathered. For those interested in viewing more historic Kailua photos, refer to *Kailua,* the excellent new book by the Kailua Historical Society. The captions, in keeping with the nature of this book, are very brief.

Bishop Museum: pp. xviii, 5, 11, 21, 56, 95, 104, 117, 161 (right), 162 (both)
City & County of Honolulu: pp. 36, 63
Erling William Hedemann, Jr.: p. 18
George and Lynn Abe Family Collection: p. xii
Geri Ihara: p. 22
Hawai'i State Archives: pp. 80, 90, 96, 103, 110, 138
Honolulu Star-Bulletin: pp. xiv, 6, 54, 64, 118, 161 (left), 163 (left)
Jackie Young Collection: p. 160 (right)
Kim Martin: p. 163 (right)
Miyaji Family (Trudi Miyaji): p. 9
Samuel Lee Collection: p. 160 (left)

About the Author

Born and raised in Hawai'i, Sandra Park now lives in California, teaching at Ohlone College and other Bay Area schools. She received her BA from the University of Hawai'i, an MA in English and MFA in creative writing at San Francisco State University. An excerpt of this novella appeared in *The Iowa Review* as a fiction award runner-up. She received an AWP Fellowship in Prague, Czech Republic and SLS Scholarship in St. Petersburg, Russia. <www.sandratpark.com>